MW01247566

AUDACIOUS WOMEN

AN ANTHOLOGY

Edited by Reine Dugas, Lauren Rachel Berman,
and the HRM Editorial Collective

HOT REDHEAD
MEDIA
ALL THINGS BOOKS AND LIT

Reprinted Work:

"The Linda Wolfe Poem" by Joel Allegretti. First published in Platypus by Joel Allegretti. NYQ Books, 2017.

"Unimpressed with Offenbach, Weary of Rilke, Perplexed by Cocteau, but Amused by Black Orpheus, Eurydice Reveals Herself to Be the Original Greta Garbo" and "Poem for Nico" by Joel Allegretti. First published in Father Silicon by Joel Allegretti, The Poet's Press, 2006.

"Woman on the Beach" by Joel Allegretti. First published in The Same, Winter/Spring 2011, Volume 8, Number 2.

"A Respectable Woman" by Kate Chopin. First published in Vogue, February 15, 1894.

"Simple Glasses" by Avital Gad-Cykman. First published in Light Reflection Over Blues: Short Prose, Ravenna Press, 2022.

"The War Still Within" by Tanya Ko Hong. First published in The War Still Within, KYSO Flash, 2019.

"Do you still believe in spring?" by Tanya Ko Hong. First published in Metro, Art Card Project, "WE, OUR,US", 2021.

"Waiting" by Tanya Ko Hong. First published in Palos Verdes Library Anthology in 2015.

"Drenched in Light" by Zora Neale-Hurston. First published in Opportunity, December 1924.

"Is This a Joke?" by Leslie Pietrzyk. First published in Southern Indiana Review, Volume 28, Number 1, Spring 2021, 57-60.

"Talunang Manok" by Marivi Soliven. First published in Everyday Genius, December 11, 2014.

"Before the moon I am, what a woman is, a woman of power, a woman's power, deeper than the roots of trees, deeper than the roots of islands, older than the Making, older than the moon."
—Ursula K. Le Guin

TABLE OF CONTENTS

EDITORS' FOREWORD

The idea for this anthology came from coffee dates and conversations about women, between women, on the topic of wanting to see more creative work that embraced the concept of women fully occupying their spaces, developing agency, and trailblazing powerful futures. The six person Hot Redhead Media editorial team invited submissions from authors and artists of all genders and orientations, making the simple yet complicated ask: Can you share some creative work for our publication that lets women both be true to their authentic strength and allow for the vibe to be smart and celebratory, letting us laugh, cry, muse, and think deeply about the ways in which women come to this world as influencers?

We sought work in art, poems, plays, creative non-fiction, and fiction that embraced the concept of women with complexity, multi-dimensionality, and that strange and gorgeous luster known as female autonomy, wanting to both borrow from the past (by including authors like Kate Chopin and Zora Neale Hurston)—and to take the female audacity into the future. This anthology begins with a famous public domain story "Drenched in Light," by Zora Neale Hurston, published in 1924 and recently entered into public domain, that features the sassiest and boldest little girl any of us had ever read, where Neale Hurston makes Isie Watts, by her own admission, her character study of her happy Southern childhood. It then moves to an accomplished flash fiction story called "Simple Glasses," by Israeli author Avital Gad-Cykman that illustrates a compelling, non-toxic father-daughter love, wherein a father teaches his little girl to see through the lens of deliberate positivity.

When authors champion men taking stands that uplift women improve agency for women, we applaud. We'd like to see more characters of that nature enter the sphere of celebrated literary work and common image reperatoire. "Audacious women" thus has a wide definition and the work selected displays a variety of takes and views. Too, we were pleased to include poems from Joel Allegretti that featured women who were desired long after they left a beach, women stating and taking their need for independence, women with "derelict" hearts, and women who recognized the injustices done to other women and tried to resolve them. We feature the irreverent and wonderful "Holy Inappropriate" short play by Allison Fradkin that parses the ways religion creates and dismantles gender roles and champions how women must create their own rebellions to own rights to their reproductive organs. Cue in the Biblical Cliteralists!

Something particularly compelling in some work selected was   representation of archetypes of women as healers and mages, but also compelling was the idea of women rebels. From Marivi Soliven's story "Talunang Manok" about a marital relationship where a deceived wife uses her culinary skills to enact powerful vengeance to Galel Medina's surreal piece "Concepcion," where the devil is sexy and female, the authors in these pages do not pull their punches.

With works in this anthology that three-dimensionally parse women's relationships with their families, careers, histories, societal expectations, and erotic choices from these and other featured authors, we hope that what is in these pages excites you as much as it excited us. Every author selected here ignited a hopeful spark and we thank them for their contributions. The visual artists featured here also lifted our spirits and elevated our view of female audacity. With a spirit of inquiry, this project began. With a spirit of inquiry, it goes out. Now, we offer it to you, dear reader.

We hope that you, too, are drenched in light and wonder. With endearing love and respect for audacious girls and women everywhere, we make this offering. Please enjoy.

With thanks for your support and readership,
Reine Dugas, Lauren R. Berman, and the HRM Editorial Board

DRENCHED IN LIGHT
by Zora Neale Hurston

Y ou Isie Watts! Git 'own offen dat gate post an' rake up dis yahd!"

The little brown figure perched upon the gate post looked yearningly up the gleaming shell road that led to Orlando, and down the road that led to Sanford and shrugged her thin shoulders. This heaped kindling on Grandma Potts' already burning ire.

"Lawd a-mussy!" she screamed, enraged—"Heah Joel, gimme dat wash stick. Ah'll show dat limb of Satan she kain't shake huhseff at me. If she ain't down by de time Ah gets dere, Ah'll break huh down in de lines" (loins).

"Aw Gran'ma, Ah see Mist' George and Jim Robinson comin' and Ah wanted to wave at 'em," the child said petulantly.

"You jes wave dat rake at dis heah yahd, madame, else Ah'll take you down a button hole lower. You'se too 'oomanish jumpin' up in every-body's face dat pass."

This struck the child in a very sore spot for nothing pleased her so much as to sit atop of the gate post and hail the passing vehicles on their way South to Orlando, or North to Sanford. That white shell road was her great attraction. She raced up and down the stretch of it that lay before her gate like a round eyed puppy hailing gleefully all travelers. Everybody in the country, white and colored, knew little Isis Watts, the joyful. The Robinson brothers, white cattlemen, were particularly fond of her and always extended a stirrup for her to climb up behind one of them for a short ride, or let her try to crack the long bull whips and yee whoo at the cows.

Grandma Potts went inside and Isis literally waved the rake at the "chaws" of ribbon cane that lay so bountifully about the yard in company with the knots and peelings, with a thick sprinkling of peanut hulls.

The herd of cattle in their envelope of gray dust came alongside and Isis dashed out to the nearest stirrup and was lifted up.

"Hello theah Snidlits, I was wonderin' wheah you was," said Jim Robinson as she snuggled down behind him in the saddle. They were almost out of the danger zone when Grandma emerged.

"You Isie-s!" she bawled.

The child slid down on the opposite side from the house and executed a flank movement through the corn patch that brought her into the yard from behind the privy.

"You Iii' hasion you! Wheah you been?"

"Out in de back yahd," Isis lied and did a cart wheel and a few fancy steps on her way to the front again.

"If you doan git tuh dat yahd, Ah make a mommuk of you!" Isis observed that Grandma was cutting a fancy assortment of switches from peach, guana and cherry trees.

She finished the yard by raking everything under the edge of the porch and began a romp with the dogs, those lean, floppy eared 'coon hounds that all country folks keep. But Grandma vetoed this also.

"Isie, you set 'own on dat porch! Uh great big 'leben yeah ole gal racin' an' rompin' lak dat—set 'own!"

Isis impatiently flung herself upon the steps.

"Git up offa dem steps, you aggavatin' limb, 'fore Ah git dem hick'ries tuh you, an' set yo' seff on a cheah."

Isis petulently arose and sat down as violently as possible in a chair, but slid down until she all but sat upon her shoulder blades.

"Now look atcher," Grandma screamed. "Put yo' knees together, an' git up often yo' backbone! Lawd, you know dis hellion is gwine make me stomp huh insides out."

Isis sat bolt upright as if she wore a ramrod down her back and began to whistle. Now there are certain things that Grandma Potts felt no one of this female persuasion should do—one was to sit with the knees separated, "settin' brazen" she called it; another was whistling, another playing with boys, neither must a lady cross her legs.

Up she jumped from her scat to get the switches.

"So yousc whistlin' in mah face, huh!" She glared till her eyes were beady and Isis bolted for safety. But the noon hour brought John Watts, the widowed father, and this excused the child from sitting for criticism.

Being the only girl in the family, of course she must wash the dishes, which she did in intervals between frolics with the dogs. She even gave Jake, the puppy, a swim in the dishpan by holding him suspended above the water that reeked of "pot likker"—just high enough so that his feet would be immersed. The deluded puppy swam and swam without ever crossing the pan, much to his annoyance. Hearing Grandma she hurriedly dropped him on the floor, which he tracked up with feet wet with dishwater.

Grandma took her patching and settled down in the front room to sew. She did this every afternoon, and invariably slept in the big red rocker with her head lolled back over the back, the sewing falling from her hand.

Isis had crawled under the center table with its red plush cover with little round balls for fringe. She was lying on her back imagining herself various personages. She wore trailing robes, golden slippers with blue bottoms. She rode white horses with flaring pink nostrils to the horizon, for she still believed that to be land's end. She was picturing herself gazing over the edge of the world into the abyss when the spool of cotton fell from Grandma's lap and rolled away under the whatnot. Isis drew back from her contemplation of the nothingness at the horizon and glanced up at the sleeping woman. Her head had fallen far back. She breathed with a regular "snark" intake and soft "poosah" exhaust. But Isis was a visual minded child. She heard the snores only subconsciously but she saw straggling beard on Grandma's chin, trembling a little with every "snark" and "poosah". They were long gray hairs curled here and there against the dark brown skin. Isis was moved with pity for her mother's mother.

"Poah Gran-ma needs a shave," she murmured, and set about it. Just then Joel, next older than Isis, entered with a can of bait.

"Come on Isie, les' we all go fishin'. The perch is bitin' fine in Blue Sink."

"Sh-sh— " cautioned his sister, "Ah got to shave Gran'ma."

"Who say so?" Joel asked, surprised.

"Nobody doan hafta tell me. Look at her chin. No ladies don't weah no whiskers if they kin help it. But Gran'ma gittin' ole an' she doan know how to shave like me."

The conference adjourned to the back porch lest Grandma wake.

"Aw, Isie, you doan know nothin' 'bout shavin' a-tall—but a man lak me—"

"Ah do so know."

"You don't not. Ah'm goin' shave her mahseff."

"Naw, you won't neither, Smarty. Ah saw her first an' thought it all up first," Isis declared, and ran to the calico covered box on the wall above the wash basin and seized her father's razor. Joel was quick and seized the mug and brush.

"Now!" Isis cried defiantly, "Ah got the razor."

"Goody, goody, goody, pussy cat, Ah got th' brush an' you can't shave 'thout lather—see! Ah know mo' than you," Joel retorted.

"Aw, who don't know dat?" Isis pretended to scorn. But seeing her progress blocked for lack of lather she compromised.

"Ah know! Les' we all shave her. You lather an' Ah shave." This was agreeable to Joel. He made mountains of lather and anointed his own chin, and the chin of Isis and the dogs, splashed the walls and at last was persuaded to lather Grandma's chin. Not that he was loath but he wanted his new plaything to last as long as possible.

Isis stood on one side of the chair with the razor clutched cleaver fashion. The niceties of razor-handling had passed over her head. The thing with her was to hold the razor sufficient in itself.

Joel splashed on the lather in great gobs and Grandma awoke.

For one bewildered moment she stared at the grinning boy with the brush and mug but sensing another presence, she turned to behold the business face of Isis and the razor clutching hand. Her jaw dropped and Grandma, forgetting years and rheumatism, bolted from the chair and fled the house, screaming.

"She's gone to tell papa, Isie. You didn't have no business wid his razor and he's gonna lick yo hide," Joel cried, running to replace the mug and brush.

"You too, chuckle-head, you, too," retorted Isis. "You was playin' wid his brush and put it all over the dogs-Ah seen you put it on Ned an' Beulah." Isis shaved some slivers from the door jamb with the razor and replaced it in the box. Joel took his bait and pole and hurried to Blue Sink. Isis crawled under the house to brood over the whipping she knew would come. She had meant well.

But sounding brass and tinkling cymbal drew her forth. The local lodge of the Grand United Order of Odd Fellows led by a braying, thudding band, was marching in full regalia down the road. She had forgotten the barbecue and log rolling to be held today for the benefit of the new hall.

Music to Isis meant motion. In a minute razor and whipping forgotten, she was doing a fair imitation of the Spanish dancer she had seen in a medicine show some time before. Isis' feet were gifted—she could dance most anything she saw.

Up, up went her spirits, her brown little feet doing all sorts of intricate things and her body in rhythm, hand curving above her head. But the music was growing faint. Grandma was nowhere in sight. She stole out of the gate, running and dancing after the band.

Then she stopped. She couldn't dance at the carnival. Her dress was torn and dirty. She picked a long stemmed daisy and thrust it behind her ear. But the dress, no better. Oh, an idea! In the battered round topped trunk in the bedroom!

She raced back to the house, then, happier, raced down the white dusty road to the picnic grove, gorgeously clad. People laughed good naturedly at her, the band played and Isis danced because she couldn't help it. A crowd of children gathered admiringly about her as she wheeled lightly about, hand on hip, flower between her teeth with the red and white fringe of the table-cloth—Grandma's new red tablecloth that she wore in lieu of a Spanish shawl—trailing in the dust. It was too ample for her meager form, but she wore it like a gipsy. Her brown feet twinkled in and out of the fringe. Some grown people joined the children about her. The Grand Exalted Ruler rose to speak; the band was hushed, but Isis danced on, the crowd clapping their hands for her. No one listened to the Exalted one, for little by little the multitude had surrounded the brown dancer.

An automobile drove up to the Crown and halted. Two white men and a lady got out and pushed into the crowd, suppressing mirth discreetly behind gloved hands. Isis looked up and waved them a magnificent hail and went on dancing until—

Grandma had returned to the house and missed Isis and straight-way sought her at the festivities expecting to find her in her soiled dress, shoeless, gaping at the crowd, but what she saw drove her frantic. Here was her granddaughter dancing before a gaping crowd in her brand new red tablecloth, and reeking of lemon extract, for Isis had added the final touch to her costume. She must have perfume.

Isis saw Grandma and bolted. She heard her cry: "Mah Gawd, mah brand new table cloth Ah jus' bought f'um O'landah!" as she fled through the crowd and on into the woods

II

She followed the little creek until she came to the ford in a rutty wagon road that led to Apopka and laid down on the cool grass at the roadside. The April sun was quite hot.

Misery, misery and woe settled down upon her and the child wept. She knew another whipping was in store for her.

"Oh, Ah wish Ah could die, then Gran'ma an' papa would be sorry they beat me so much. Ah b'leeve Ah'll run away an' never go home no mo'. Ah'm goin' drown mahscff in th' creek!" Her woe grew attractive.

Isis got up and waded into the water. She routed out a tiny 'gator and a huge bull frog. She splashed and sang, enjoying herself immensely. The purr of a motor struck her car and she saw a large, powerful car jolting along the rutty road toward her. It stopped at the water's edge.

"Well, I declare, it's our little gypsy," exclaimed the man at the wheel. "What are you doing here, now?"

"Ah'm killin' mahseff," Isis declared dramatically, "Cause Gran'ma beats me too much."

There was a hearty burst of laughter from the machine.

"You'll last sometime the way you are going about it. Is this the way to Maitland? We want to go to the Park Hotel."

Isis saw no longer any reason to die. She came up out of the water, holding up the dripping fringe of the tablecloth.

"Naw, indeedy. You go to Maitlan' by the shell road—it goes by mah house—an' turn off at Lake Sebelia to the clay road that takes you right to the do'."

"Well," went on the driver, smiling furtively, "Could you quit dying long enough to go with us?"

"Yessuh," she said thoughtfully, "Ah wanta go wid you."

The door of the car swung open. She was invited to a seat beside the driver. She had often dreamed of riding in one of these heavenly chariots but never thought she would, actually. "Jump in then, Madame Tragedy, and show us. We lost ourselves after we left your barbecue."

During the drive Isis explained to the kind lady who smelt faintly of violets and to the indifferent men that she was really a princess. She told them about her trips to the horizon, about the trailing gowns, the gold shoes with blue bottoms she insisted on the blue bottoms—the white charger, the time when she was Hercules and had slain numerous dragons and sundry giants. At last the car approached her gate over which stood the umbrella China-berry tree. The car was abreast of the gate and had all but passed when Grandma spied her glorious tablecloth lying back against the upholstery of the Packard.

"You Isie-e!" she bawled. "You Iii' wretch you! come heah dis instant."

"That's me," the child confessed, mortified, to the lady on the rear seat.

"Oh, Sewell, stop the car. This is where the child lives. I hate to give her up though."

"Do you wanta keep me?" Isis brightened.

"Oh, I wish I could, you shining little morsel. Wait, I'll try to save you a whipping this time."

She dismounted with the gaudy lemon flavored culprit and advanced to the gate where Grandma stood glowering, switches in hand.

"You're gointuh ketchit f'um yo' haid to yo' heels m'lady. Jes' come in heah."

"Why, good afternoon," she accosted the furious grandparent. "You're not going to whip this poor little thing, are you?" the lady asked in conciliatory tones.

"Yes, Ma'am. She's de wustest lil' limb dat ever drawed bref. Jes' look at mah new table cloth, dat ain't never been washed. She done traipsed all over de woods, uh dancin' an' uh prancin' in it. She done took a razor to me t'day an' Lawd knows whut mo'."

Isis clung to the white hand fearfully.

'Ah wuzn't gointer hurt Gran'ma, miss—Ah wuz jus' gointer shave her whiskers fuh huh 'cause she's old an' can't." The white hand closed tightly over the little brown one that was quite soiled. She could understand a voluntary act of love even though it miscarried.

"Now, Mrs. er—er—I didn't get the name—how much did your tablecloth cost?"

"One whole big silvah dollar down at O'landah—ain't had it a week yit."

"Now here's five dollars to get another one. The little thing loves laughter. I want her to go on to the hotel and dance in that tablecloth for me. I can stand a little light today—"

"Oh, yessum, yessum," Grandma cut in, "Everything's al right, sho' she kin go, yessum."

The lady went on: "I want brightness and this Isis is joy itself, why she's drenched in light!"

Isis for the first time in her life, felt herself appreciated and danced up and down in an ecstasy of joy for a minute.

"Now, behave yo'seff, Isie, ovah at de hotel wid de white folks,"

Grandma cautioned, pride in her voice, though she strove to hide it. "Lawd, ma'am, dat gal keeps me so frackshus, Ah doan know mah haid f'um mah feet. Ah orter comb huh haid, too, befo' she go wid you all."

"No, no, don't bother. I like her as she is. I don't think she'd like it either, being combed and scrubbed. Come on, Isis."

Feeling that Grandma had been somewhat squelched did not detract from Isis' spirit at all. She pranced over to the waiting motor and this time seated herself on the rear seat between the sweet, smiling lady and the rather aloof man in gray.

"Ah'm gointer stay wid you all," she said with a great deal of warmth, and snuggled up to her benefactress. "Want me tuh sing a song fuh you?"

"There, Helen, you've been adopted," said the man with a short, harsh laugh.

"Oh, I hope so, Harry." She put her arm about the red draped figure at her side and drew it close until she felt the warm puffs of the child's breath against her side. She looked hungrily ahead of her and spoke into space rather than to anyone in the car. "I want a little of her sunshine to soak into my soul. I need it."

"Nesting" by Kelsey Bryan-Zwick

SIMPLE GLASSES
by Avital Gad Cykman

Last week after the first rain, I almost stepped on a shamrock while taking a shortcut to the bus station through an open field. A rich scent emanated from the damp soil with something like anticipation blistered with bubbles. I was tempted but did not pluck the clover because, back in the field that miraculously survived the intense construction of ugly buildings in our neighborhood, you told me not to. You and I squatted beside the little plant, a father and a child, and you squeezed your eyes behind your eyeglasses as you studied the shamrock and told me it is an Irish sign, and if it had four leaves it would also mean good luck.

We observed the vegetation together.

"I don't see any four-leafed ones," I said. "Here, take my eyeglasses," you said.

You tucked them behind my ears and pressed them against the bridge of my nose. The world blurred, and my knees buckled from dizziness just as they did when I fell once and suffered a concussion and you came running to pick me up.

I couldn't tell whether I saw three or four leaves. "I don't see how many!" I said, laughing awkwardly.

"So, you must be looking at a four-leaf shamrock," you said. "Now, let's go buy you a bagel at Baruch's kiosk, and I'll have a strong black coffee."

We drink such coffee in simple glasses every day now, you in my dreams and me, at home. Your eyeglasses serve us both, although I have my own. The melon I see is the sweetest. My love is the most beautiful. A shamrock always grows with four leaves.

꧁꧂

FIVE POEMS
by Joel Allegretti

Woman on the Beach
After a print by Georg Baselitz

Wishful thinking, friend.
But she is gone from the beach,
Has fled dry soil, is blended with the blue.
Only her silhouette in the sand remains,
And after high tide rinses dusk,
Our memory of the silhouette.

She wants no part of our lives,
Prefers sunlight below the surface,
Remembers sea-swept midnights.
She has Gauguin's Tahitians on her mind
And wants to see for herself
What she has been taught all her life:

There are always more pearls
In the ocean than on the land.

☙❧

Unimpressed with Offenbach, Weary of Rilke, Perplexed by Cocteau, Though Amused by *Black Orpheus*, Eurydice Reveals Herself to Be the Original Greta Garbo

From Night I came.
To Night I went.
In Night I belong.
You have known this forever.

You lost me in the spaces between your strings.
In every grace note and scale, you embedded my name.
The nowhere I wander resonates with my name.
Every vein, every crevice of this dispiriting abyss
Is sealed with its mortar:
My name as it was sung—as it was shaped—
As it was stuttered by the voice that anguishes your throat.

Souls whirl in the windliness of Hell
And echo your cry of my name
And echo your cry of my name
And echo every curse you lay upon your failure to believe,
You—who dressed the naked shades in the rare silk
        of your singing,
You—who colored my silhouette through perpetual lamentation.

I have been telling you this
For thousands of years. What more is there to say?
Man of the Harp, tell your descendants to turn
To other fables and leave us—me, in particular—for good.

I want to be alone.

෨෬෧෮

Poem for Nico

Somehow,
There was always Berlin.

You never ceased to hear
The cranky rhythms of the trains
            —headed where?—
That rat-a-tatted little Christa to sleep,
And the Nibelungen danced
            through her dreams
            in patent-leather boots.

A record whirls
On a parlor phonograph:

Hildegard Knef singing
"Song of the Lonely Girl"
            in 1952.
            You hated her.
Thirty years on,
In the pale blue fluorescence
            of flame under spoon,
You would think
            she sounds like you.

Always an inch away,
Vicious as a razor,
            dark as your *Sturm und* drone:
The dreadful edge
            you hungered for.

Your guide was not the murdered father;
The mad mother walking circles
        round the kitchen;
The neglectful lovers;
Or the absent, present, absent son.

I don't tempt fate. Fate tempts me.

The derelict heart beats out of time.

৩৩৩৯

The Linda Wolfe Poem
*A resident of Anderson, Indiana, who holds
the world record for most-married woman*

I do believe I meant "I do" the first time I said "I do"
and discovered I didn't mean "I do" and thought my
second "I do" would be my last "I do," but another
"I do" was in the cards, followed by a fourth "I do,"
and then a fifth, and then … I do like the words "I do"
and am more adept at saying "I do" than others are at
saying "I do," if I do say so myself, because I've said
"I do" even more than Zsa Zsa, who multiplied "I do"
by nine, and I do have to admit that I do think of her
as an "I do" amateur. Yes, I do. I do hope my latest
"I do" will be my final "I do." Really, I do.

৩৩৩৯

Memphis Minnie's Unmarked Grave

I might tell everybody what that Chickasaw has done, done for me,
I might tell everybody what that Chickasaw has done, done for me,
She done stole my man away and blowed that doggone smoke on me,
She's a low-down dirty dog.
                    Memphis Minnie
                    "Chickasaw Train Blues (Low Down Dirty Thing)"

Lizzie Douglas sang. Yes, she did. She didn't train out of here on the Chickasaw caboose. No, a stroke robbed her nursing-home pillow in 1973. A synonym for stroke is brain attack. "When brain cells die during a stroke, abilities controlled by that area of the brain are lost. How a stroke patient is affected depends on where the stroke occurs in the brain and how much the brain is damaged."[1] Lizzie was born in Louisiana and performed for loose change on Memphis streets before the microphone transferred her singing to 78 RPM records. They say she played guitar like a man. Her remains lie in a Baptist cemetery in Mississippi, birthplace of Tennessee Williams. A headstone honored Tennessee's grave right after his burial. Lizzie got hers twenty-three years after her death (she was a Negro, you know), courtesy of Bonnie Raitt. Thank you, Bonnie.

ༀ☉ༀ

---

[1] National Stroke Association

HOLY INAPPROPRIATE
by Allison Fradkin

SYNOPSIS

Here's the story of a lovely lady who is bringing up three very lovely girls...
in the Christian Patriarchy Movement. All of them have been controlled,
like their mother, by their heavenly father. Mother's little helpers know
very well that their mission in life is submission and that womanhood is
synonymous with motherhood. Now that all three are officially members
of the premarital sex, it's time for Mom to teach them about the birds and
the believers. But what happens when she discovers that the disciples at
her disposal are neither disposable nor...dispassionate?

CHARACTERS

Mary Jo, the mother

a godly woman delightfully devoted to her family and her faith, Mary
Jo is the epitome of bonhomie; however, she is starting to feel the effects
of sexual repression and is beginning to experience misgivings about her
conservative convictions and limiting lifestyle

Damaris, the youngest daughter

bored with the Lord, Damaris possesses character traits that are incon-
gruous with her upbringing: verbosity and curiosity; she's certain there's
more to life than caretaking and baby-making and resists her family's insis-
tence on infants and infantilization

Tamar, the middle daughter

the genuinely genial and innocently inquisitive Tamar acts as placater and
peacemaker; taking her cues from both her younger and older sisters, she
is at once ambivalent and ambiguous, as well as effortlessly humorous

Lois, the eldest daughter

ignorantly blissful and impishly imperious, Lois's indoctrination into her
family's belief system is so successful, she can run purity rings around any
and every fundamentalist female in existence; she can't wait to create a
family—and an army—for God

*The daughters' ages are unspecified because they are all considered "girls" until
marriage and motherhood—and even then, they don't necessarily lose that
label.*

*All aspects of the family's appearance—from hairdos to modest attire to the
girls' prominent purity rings—obliterate their individuality. Yet while the
characters should lack color sartorially, the cast itself should not be comparably
colorless—or even monochromatic.*

SETTING
A home classroom that feels more like a waiting room.

TIME
The present.

At rise, DAMARIS, TAMAR, and LOIS stand in a circular formation
beneath child-size umbrellas under the watchful eye of MARY JO, whose
countenance conveys that she is pensive and apprehensive, yet also astute
and resolute.

ALL

*(singing, the tune an amusing amalgam of "Jesus Loves Me" and "Lizzie
Borden Took an Ax")*

In our ring of purity / We enjoy immunity / From hell and maturity / And
best of all, equality

DAMARIS

I still don't have a handle on this.

TAMAR

You're holding it, goofball.

DAMARIS

Must we take everything literally?

LOIS

Yes, Damaris. We are *(enthusiastically enunciating)* Biblical Literalists.

MARY JO

You have received this covering because you are now officially a member of
the premarital sex.

LOIS

The Umbrella of Protection is God's most perfect design. With Him as top
banana and Dad as second banana, you will never slip up and imperil your
innocence—as long as you don't slip out from under their canopy of care.

MARY JO

Happy Your-Body-Can-Now-Give-Birth Day, Damaris, which it is prepared
to do no earlier than nine months to the day of your wedding day. *(taking hold
of Damaris's left hand)* This halo on your ring finger is not only a gift from
your father. It is a constant reminder of your decision to reserve reproduction
for marriage. *(patting Damaris's pelvis)* Eggers can't be choosers. Right, girls?

(Lois and Tamar ad-lib their agreement.)
Now, make like a woman in church and shut it.
(The girls close their umbrellas and take a seat.)
The topic of today's mother-daughter fellowship is... Wait for it.
(Mary Jo turns her attention to a magnetic alphabet board and begins locating the letters that comprise MATURATION.)

LOIS

Oh, I will wait, Mother. Without question, I will wait!

DAMARIS

Jeez, Lois, will you quit throwing your "wait" around?

LOIS

Absolutely not, Damaris. Pure and simple, I am proud to be pure—and simple.

TAMAR

But isn't pride a sin?

LOIS

Only when it's expressed by a homosexual.
(Tamar's face conveys that she feels personally attacked by this remark.)
God lets my pride slide. Like an engagement ring onto a finger. A girl can dream, can't she?

DAMARIS

That's about all she can do.

MARY JO

And that, Damaris, is enough.

DAMARIS

Sorry, Mom.

TAMAR

Maybe what Mommy means is that dreaming is more than sufficient.

LOIS

I do get a lot of pleasure out of it.

MARY JO

Well, it has to come from somewhere. Uh, which is why we will be discussing...
(Mary Jo gestures to the alphabet board, on which she has succeeded in spelling out MATURATION.)

LOIS

Maturation? But that's another word for evolution. Creationism is a compulsory component of a Christ-centered homeschool curriculum.

MARY JO

Then it will comfort you to know that our focus is on sexual maturation: *(presenting a basket of pint-sized baby dolls)* the process by which our bodies enable us to *create* life.

LOIS

Ooh, if I can put all my fertilized eggs in one basket, that must mean I can put all my *un*fertilized eggs in *two* baskets, thereby doubling down on not denying my unborn children the right to life.

LOIS (c'td)

Oh, thank God. *(closes her eyes in supplication)* Thank you, God. *(opens her eyes)* And thank you, Mother. You used that board to teach us how to read, and now you're going to use it to teach us how to breed. This is so full circle. I love it.

MARY JO

I admire your zealotry, Lois. However, it might surprise you to know that a baby is not a woman's only bundle of joy.

(She introduces a rudimentary replica of female genitalia: a piggybank with a pompom ball tacked near the tip of its exposed coin slot, which could be curtained by crushed velvet. She points out the pompom.)

She also has this one, generously applied to her sex organs—specifically, the vulva; more specifically, the labia minora. This God-given gift is called Clitoris. Repeat after me: Cli-*tor*-is.

GIRLS

Cli-*tor*-is.

MARY JO

Like you girls, Clitoris has a servant's heart. Each and every one of its nerves serves the sole purpose of providing you with joy.

TAMAR

That is so angelic.

LOIS

Not as angelic as I am. Well, except when it comes to...the area of...*the area*. Mother, what do I do when I experience the urge to engage in the activity that involves both joyous bundles?

MARY JO

Oh, Lois, I wish you'd confided in me about your urgency. You could've come sooner. That is, you could have come to me sooner. Those urges—those feelings of desire you're experiencing— are not unlike personal goals and higher education. They must be passionately denied. Until marriage.

DAMARIS

So if we get married, we can do all that stuff? I cannot wait to get married! I will, obviously, so good things will come to me, but at least now I actually have a reason to. I'm so glad you asked, Lois. What's the answer, Mom? What should we do to deal with our desires while we wait?

MARY JO

We look to Proverbs 31:13. "A virtuous woman worketh willingly with her hands." Doing so can make waiting both tolerable and pleasurable, perhaps even...preferable. And when the waiting period is over, you may...need to continue to engage your hands, as Jesus commands—an extension that the season of life in which you can no longer grin and child-bear it absolutely demands.

LOIS

But, Mother, the Proverbs 31 Woman is called to use faith-friendly fibers in the construction of her modest attire. "She seeketh wool and flax, and worketh willingly with her hands." Taking the characteristics of a virtuous woman out of context, taking anything in the Good Book out of context, is—

DAMARIS

Something we do religiously. You'd know that if you ever read another book.

LOIS

Oh, like you do? When you sneak off to the library?

DAMARIS

Yeah, well, some of us would rather be readers than breeders, eggheads than pregheads—

LOIS

Mother, did you know about this? That she goes to the library? The *lie*-brary, Mother. It's right there in the word!

TAMAR

Are you saying The Word is a lie, especially the part about man lying with... you-know-who?

DAMARIS

My, my, Lois. I had no idea you had such an impious pie-hole.

MARY JO
(not entirely displeased) Girls, we are getting out of bounds—

LOIS
Then it's a good thing we're still out of earshot. We *are* still out of earshot, aren't we? *(gasps)* I hear Father's footsteps!
> *(Each of them reacts to the prospect of their father's approach: Lois with sincere fear, Tamar with ambivalence, Damaris with annoyance, Mary Jo with a mixture of fright and delight.)*

There they are. King-size, sandal-sheathed, soul-saving footsteps arriving to Leviti-cuss us out—minus the profanity, of course.

DAMARIS
The only thing more fertile than your womb, sis, is your imagination.
> *(The girls ad-lib their disagreement over the threat to their safety.)*

MARY JO
Girls, let's resume our lesson, please. I promise you we're safe—for now. Girls. Girls, no one is coming until you learn how!
> *(An explosion of silence follows Mary Jo's outburst.)*

DAMARIS
Great, now you've upset Mom. Nice going, *Lowest.*

LOIS
Hey! *(pelts Damaris with a baby from the basket of infinitesimal infants)* Only the boys are allowed to call me that, *Demerit.*

DAMARIS
Oh, yeah? Why?

LOIS
(as she pelts Damaris with more diminutive dolls) When they do it, it's chivalrous. They're just reminding me of my place, of my mission in life,

which is submission. When you do it, it's unacceptable, unladylike, and ungodly.

> *(Now all three girls get in on the baby shower, which devolves into a cross between the American Gladiators Assault Event and the Double Dare Physical Challenge. Intensified by improvised exclamations of encouragement and discouragement, this Fundamentalist spin on a food fight shows us that Lois does not "throw like a girl." In fact, she almost single-handedly transforms the shower into a brutish contact sport.)*

MARY JO

Girls, stop!

> *(Damaris and Tamar instantly obey. Lois does not.)*

My word, Lois, I really had no idea you were fearfully and wonderfully made of sterner stuff. You've never disobeyed me before.

> *(It's an astonishment, not an admonishment, and it stops Lois cold.)*

Praise be!

DAMARIS

Not only were you astoundingly aggressive, Lois; you were positively progressive!

LOIS

I was?

TAMAR

Yeah, you totally... Wait, what's "gressive"? I know we're pro-life, pro-death penalty, pro-family. But we've never been pro-gressive. Have we?

LOIS

No, we have not. And we aren't going to start now. Therefore, I apologize profusely for allowing my desire for...for...for motherhood to override my feminine virtues.

MARY JO

It wasn't your desire for motherhood, Lois. It was your desire for self-control. More accurately, your desire to have control over yourself. This condition—no, this state of existence—is called *(spelling it out on the alphabet board)* autonomy.

LOIS

Autonomy, huh? That could be...that could be liberating!

DAMARIS

Now there's a thought!

LOIS

I just had a thought? I just had a thought? I just had a thought! I, a female human, gave birth to a concept. Mother, did you know that liberation could be freeing?

MARY JO

Well, you know what we say: Life begins at conception.

TAMAR

But isn't thinking unthinkable for someone of our sex?

MARY JO

That is...also something we believe. It's what our faith teaches us—that not unlike piggybanks, those in possession of them cannot think or even speak for themselves. On the other hand...piggybanks can make change, and we have piggybanks.

DAMARIS

So...we can make change?

LOIS

We can?

TAMAR

(to Mary Jo) Yeah, Mommy, can we?

LOIS

No, we cannot. That would be...that would be revolutionary. Revolu-*tion*-ary. With extra special emphasis on shun. Because that's exactly what everyone will do to us, including our heavenly father—not to mention God.

MARY JO

You're right, Lois. It would be the end of our world as we know it, and to know it is to... To know that and to not share that knowledge with...with who you love, these...these darling disciples at my disposal. Except you're not disposable. And neither am I. Girls, I have come to the conclusion that there is only one correct course of action to take here: an exodus.

DAMARIS

You mean get out from under the Umbrella of Protection? Plus a few thumbs?

MARY JO

It seems that would indeed be a plus for us, girls, as it's becoming very clear to me that in its present form, our belief system is *not* called radical fundamentalism because it's exceptionally awesome. It's just...exceptionally awful.

LOIS

I think you're thinking of radical feminism.

MARY JO

You are so thoughtful for a change. Girls, you know how, when I visit with each of you individually for an hour every week—Damaris at the library, Lois in the nursery, Tamar in the closet—and you make like your umbrellas and open up? Now it's my turn. It should interest you all to know that your mother—that I, Mary Jo—once identified as a radical feminist. I tried to change things for piggybanked people, but I couldn't change them fast enough. Rather than practice patience as I advise you to do, I convinced myself that progress and equality and all that radical stuff would never...reach maturation. I decided being helpless was preferable to feeling hopeless. When I go to extremes, girls...well, I go to extremes. Lois, do you hear any footsteps?

(Lois listens carefully, then responds in the negative.)

Good, because in the wrong hands, this parasol could impair us all.

(She introduces a not-so-virginal version of the Umbrella of Protection festooned with a plethora of prophylactics and accessorized with stickers bearing momentous messages, e.g. "No Means No," "We Can Do It," "Love Is Love," "Girls Just Wanna Have Fundamental Human Rights," "Thou Shalt Not Mess With Women's Rights—Fallopians 1:22")

This, girls, is what a real Umbrella of Protection looks like. I constructed this in college for a campus-wide sexual health fair. Someone called a condom a raincoat and I got inspired. Recently, I re-decked it out, just in case I found the fortitude to be...comparably compelling.

LOIS

You went to college? With condoms? What's a condom?

MARY JO

Nature's way of saying that birth control is not exerted solely by God.

TAMAR

Wow! I want to know what "Love Is Love" means!

MARY JO

It means that no matter who you love, Tamar, God and I love you right back. Anything else would be unthinkable.

LOIS

Yeah, like an exodus. We're not really going to save ourselves from something other than marriage. I mean, *for* something other than marriage. Are we?

MARY JO

Lois, how did it feel when you disobeyed me?

LOIS

Oh, it felt pleasurable. Without question.

MARY JO

That, my dear, is an indication of maturation. However, there is still pleasure to be...harvested from submission, if the subject of that submission is
your desires.
> *(She crosses to the alphabet board and willingly works the letters S and*
> *B into MATURATION to spell MASTURBATION.)*

Heed your need, girls. Don't wait to partake in pure pleasure. *(picking up the*
piggybank) For a righteously rapturous experience, simply...

> *(Mary Jo demonstrates masturbation. The moment is cathartic, euphoric,*
> *and seriously stirring. She passes the piggybank to Damaris, who handles*
> *it with care. Damaris passes it to Tamar, who handles it with flair.)*

LOIS

Hey, quit hogging it! *(plucks the piggybank out of Tamar's hands)* Wait! Will
masturbation result in pregnancy?

MARY JO

No, but don't let that stop you.
> *(After a brief hesitation, Lois embarks on a thorough and thoroughly*
> *exultant exploration.)*

I hate to rain on your charade, Lois, but *(points to the piggybank's pompom)*
this, not the Umbrella of Protection, is God's most perfect design. Did you
enjoy your release, dear?

LOIS

Release? But that's another word for freedom. We're back to that again? This is so full circle. I love it.

MARY JO

Be sure to make those full circles on your clitoris. Where there's lubrication, there's liberation. Now, who can name the different types of freedom?

TAMAR

Religious!

DAMARIS

Of speech!

MARY JO

Of course! And then there is perhaps the most desirable freedom of all: reproductive. Now that *all* of your bodies are performing regular pregnancy preparations, I have to double down on not denying my born children the right to life. *(affixes the letter C to the board)* C is for—

TAMAR

(dreamily) Clitoris, whom I adore-is. I hope other girls have them too.

MARY JO

Oh, they do, and they're going to be very grateful that you choose to use it. Which brings me back to—C is also for Choice.

DAMARIS

So we can *choose* freedom? In all its euphoric forms?
        (Lois begins to pray silently.)
We can...create our own convictions and values and rules?

MARY JO

I've always been pro creation. Sooner or later, I'll be positively progressive again.

DAMARIS

But what about our non-God dad? And our brothers?

MARY JO

We're going to share with them what's in our hearts and on our minds. Not immediately, but in due time. Now that we're on our way to becoming thoroughly thoughtful individuals, we have to think this through carefully and prayerfully. This is, after all, a thought-provoking...provocation. Naturally, your father will wish to pray about it as well, much like Lois is doing. I know you're scared, girls. I am too. But if we stick to it, stick it out, and stick together, we will achieve liberation, so help me God. On second thought, don't help me, God. I've got this. We've got this.

(Lois opens her eyes. Mary Jo holds up her Umbrella of Protection.)

I need everyone under my canopy of care, please.

(Damaris and Tamar joyfully join her. Lois hangs back.)

Come to Mama, ya little neophyte.

LOIS

Neophyte. That means beginner. Just like neonate means newborn. While I was praying, God opened my eyes. He said: Just follow in Mother's footsteps. But Mother said I shouldn't listen to her. I should make my own choices.

TAMAR

Oh, please say you're with us, Lois. Pretty please with a cherry-picked Bible verse on top?

LOIS

(to herself, as she approaches her family) Freedom is a compulsory component of life, freedom is a compulsory component of life... Oh! Here's one for you,

Tamar, about what happens when submission goes into remission: "Children are men's oppressors, and women rule over men." Isaiah 3:12. That sounds radical *and* exceptionally awesome.

DAMARIS

I'm glad you decided to join us, Lois. You can't spell "Genesis" without "sis," right? And this is our new beginning.

TAMAR

This is our origin story.

LOIS

Thank you, Mother, for...for emboldening me to explore *all* of my desires, even the ones I don't even know I have yet. And thank you, sisters, for making it safe to take the "me" out of "meek" and the meek out of me. I feel...protected.

TAMAR

I feel prepared.

DAMARIS

I feel pumped.

MARY JO

I feel...hopeful. And helpful. Now, who wants to cast off the first stone?

LOIS

I do, I do! I want to be "au"-inspiring. Autonomy-inspiring, of course.
> (*Lois removes her purity ring. Her sisters follow her lead. Next, they reprise—revise—their "Jesus Loves/Lizzie Borden" song.*)

In our heart of sisterhood...

DAMARIS

And Mom, with whom we've always stood...

MARY JO

We'll win the day, knock on wood...

TAMAR

Biblical *Lib*eralists for good!

MARY JO

That's it, girls, Bible belt it out! And this time, let's be Biblical Cliteralists. The Second Coming may belong to Christ, but the first coming belongs to you!

<u>Curtain</u>.

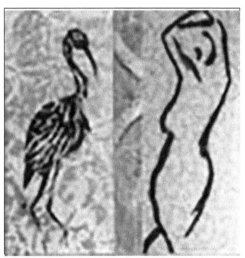

"Woman with Heron" by Cynthia Yatchman

TWO POEMS
by Traci McMickle

Bella in the Wych Elm

I was content among the branches
before the boys found me.

Looking for birds, they were.
I, a trinket, used
to line a nest.

Less than a day,
they broke their oath not to tell.

I haunted one to insanity.

During war, only soldiers are welcome
on lists of the dead.

Before a coroner,
I asked for a name
through a mouthful of taffeta.

Witch
whore
traitor

the radio said.

Drunk in the company of men.

We die too, the small people.

No one tries to find out
who we are,
nor buries us in guarded tombs
when they can't.

Remembered in graffiti.
They misplace our bones.

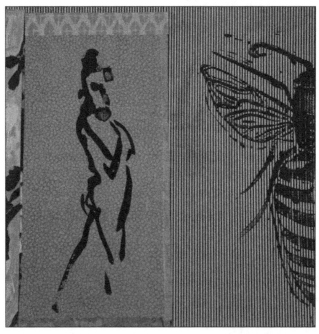

"Woman with Bee" by Cynthia Yatchman

The Closing of the Day

A widow spins
silken strands.

Her hands freeze
to the fracture point
on summer days.

When she was a girl,
her bare shoulders
defied shadows.

She misses nighttime
skies filamented with
lightning, wisps
of rain that gossamer
her hair.

What shall I make of this?

She knows her ringlets stop.
She knows her yarn begins.

She cannot tell where.

The wheel turns faster.
The fibres sting
her fingers.

Like sticks, they
kindle alive.

Her eyes are on
the window when
she hears the
mirrorcrack.

No one rode past,
but the glass
still shattered.

Her palms burn.
She looks to the river.

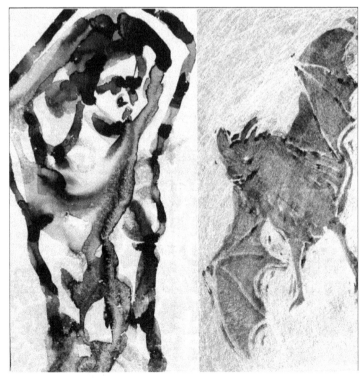

"Woman with Bat" by Cynthia Yatchman

FAMILY PHOTO
by Jen Knox

No one in our family poses for pictures, especially not my sister Diane. It's as though she thinks if there's no record of her, the real her, she won't have to worry about the impression she'll leave on this planet. I once told her that if she leaves it up to my memory and imagination, her legacy will be worse.

It's been three weeks since she disappeared. The only pictures I have of my sister are magazine adverts for perfumes and a faded print of her gingerly holding a designer clutch that costs more than my mortgage payment. I keep these photos in a shoebox under my bed, along with the few letters she wrote from the road.

There was a time I thought it cruel that my sister became the model when it had always been my dream. At ten, my primary intention was to look exactly like Linda Evangelista. I studied her, trying to decode how she could look both fifty and fourteen at the same time. I'd push up on my cheekbones until my hands hurt, aiming to embody all the female archetypes, maiden to crone, with one smile. But, alas, I was frizzy and thick-thighed and wore hexagon plastic glasses that wouldn't be considered stylish till I was thirty-five.

Only a year apart in age, I never hung out with my sister, never went goth like her, but I had great appreciation for blood-red or black lipstick and generous eyeliner. She was always bold. Looking back, The Rocky Horror Picture Show was her weekly escape. The "Time Warp" dance allowed her to uncoil her tall rigid frame. Maybe if I had gone, I'd have been there the day she was "discovered" in a downtown Cincinnati mall.

Back then, we all dreamed of being discovered because it was all we thought was available in Ohio. I tried not to get resentful as my sister traveled the world and I worked various jobs at a family-owned grocery after school. Those days, I snuck sips of Long Island Iced Tea I bought from the dead-eyed man who ran a corner store, and I imagined my sister receiving constant adoration, even though Diane always returned looking ghost-like and exhausted.

The bottle of brown liquor fit in my purse or pocket, and I shared the drink with my oddball coworkers during breaks until it was no longer fun. When my sister found my stash, she drank a full bottle in a few swallows before leaving me to swim in jealousy as she flew to Paris. She was sixteen and able to send the family sizable checks while I saw the same flat buildings and traversed the same flat roads on my way to train to be a cheesemonger for a dollar more an hour.

I wish she'd been there with me as our parents split, which they did with dedication. No phone calls, minimal correspondence. To this day, they don't speak to each other, but every passive-aggressive decision is direct communication. I suppose this is a version of love.

There was a time we all took photos together. We caught lighting bugs and found wonder in all things. I called Diane Dee Dee, and our parents were always there with a Polaroid, occasionally taking awkward selfies to get the entire family in the frame for holidays or dinners.

Today, a comprehensive photo of my estranged family would contain few enough people to ride in my SUV without crowding. I imagine the scene. All of us together in a confined space, sitting awkwardly in rows. My sister inevitably saying, "Whoever's humming, shut it." Me telling her to stop telling people what to do.

I would be driving, as I'm driving now, watching them all as I nudge the gas harder, racing beyond soy fields and diners with bottomless breakfast specials for $5.99. My stepmother tries to make small talk, and my husband offers his boisterous laugh in support. My father not-so-secretly blogs about the family road trip experience while my mother sits quietly and knits, saying sweet things and cursing under her breath.

If they were in my car now, they'd stare out opposite windows at each other's reflections.

As I stare in the rearview, I imagine the phantom road trip as though we were an ordinary family who plays trivia and laughs. My stepmom wins history. My sister nails geography. I get all the 90s entertainment questions: "Fresh Prince of Bel-Air," "Blossom," and "Golden Girls." We laugh as we remember when Mom used to dance to The Pointer Sisters in zebra prints with teased bangs.

At a stoplight on Main Street, a Whitney Houston song comes on the radio, and everything is bone silent. I am alone.

The last time my sister disappeared, she was gone six months. When she returned, I thought I had another chance to get a family photo. But real photos display too much—the silence, the jealousy, the drug-numbed gaze, the destruction. Misunderstanding. The space between words.

As I take the final turn toward home, I feel my phone buzzing and soften my gaze, remove my foot from the gas. My partner and new puppy greet me as I sink down to the floor near the front door and allow tiny teeth to gnaw at my forearm.

"Diane's in rehab. She checked herself in this time. It feels different," he says, pointing to my phone.

I scan the barrage of texts that unfold the drama. Everyone in that SUV texted me as I drove. Before I text them back, I cut an 8x10 image of my airbrushed sister from a glossy magazine and position it behind glass in a silver frame. I place it at the center of the mantel and notice my reflection beside her. For a moment, we are together again, exalted, ready to find wonder in all that's to come.

ॐ☺☺ॐ

TALUNANG MANOK
by Marivi Soliven

By the time Socorro discovered her husband was cheating on her, the affair had reached a full simmer. She had never been the sort of wife who hovered nearby when Amado took an evening call, nor did she scour his pockets for incriminating receipts. She knew that, with a husband like hers, such surveillance would have been an exercise in futility.

Amado was clever, you see. He often said, "Socorro, when it comes to white-collar crime, the smoking gun is in receipts. It's the paper trail that trips you up."

So, he never left one.

He had all cell phone bills, bank, and credit card statements mailed directly to his office. Short of breaking into the law firm's filing cabinet, she would never have learned of the daily calls to the Loft at Power Plant, the cozy dinners at Paseo Uno, the splurge on a pair of South Sea Pearl earrings that would never grace her lobes.

And yet Socorro discovered his infidelity without the confetti of a hundred trysts. She sensed something was amiss the moment his appetites changed.

*   *   *

Shortly after she began taking orders for Galantina and Pastel de Lengua, Amado mentioned that they'd been asked to host the law firm's Christmas dinner once again.

"It's that time of year, hon. Can you organize a dinner for the partners and their wives this Saturday?"

Socorro shrugged and poured herself more coffee. Organizing a 5-course sit-down dinner with wine pairings was all in a day's work for high-end caterers like her. The Secret Chef's number was on the flash dial lists of savvy Manila hostesses who had neither the ability nor the cook skilled enough to prepare Filipino haute cuisine.

"I might as well—if any of the other wives hosted the dinner, she'd hire me to cater anyway. Just remember, when you make senior partner, I'm sending them a bill for all these free meals."

Amado barely looked up from his chorizo.

"Sweetham. We get paid back every time they give me a raise, you know that."

Socorro scowled into her sinangag. She resented her husband's cavalier attitude. Although the couple had never discussed it, her catering had undoubtedly fueled Amado's rapid ascent to partner at his law firm.

The ploy that had distinguished him from the other young Turks was his habit of conducting business over dinner at home. Meals for deals, he called them. Even the most obdurate clients mellowed when negotiating contracts over Socorro's Bacalao a la Vizcaina. By the time the mango panna cotta was brought to table, his guests were completely disarmed and ready to comply with all the terms Amado had presented between first and final courses.

Word of Socorro' culinary prowess spread and the Pelaez home quickly became the preferred site for the firm's social events. On the surface, Socorro and Amado seemed to complement each other perfectly. A closer look would have revealed their marriage had begun to curdle.

*   *   *

One Saturday evening midway into Misa de Gallo season, Socorro was graciously pouring sangria for Amado's colleagues at Samson, Punzalan and Santuico, the Manila affiliate of a major New York law firm. The partners were all middle-aged executives with modest paunches, discreet comb-overs and respectable golf handicaps. Each lawyer affected an air of jovial authority that enabled him to be alternately reassuring or threatening when dealing with clients or opposing counsel.

There was more variety when it came to the wives. Soledad Punzalan was an outspoken marketing executive who had recently returned from a trip abroad sporting an alarmingly taut, heart-shaped face. Lillia Samson was a peach of a matron who directed a preschool for the progeny of Manila's best families. Bea Santuico was a Bacolod mestiza who created fanciful jewelry from excavated gold and semi-precious gems.

Socorro had never felt completely at ease with these women for unlike their families, hers was neither old—nor even newly rich. Even as her catering business gave her access into their rarefied social circles, it also put her in the awkward position of being both guest and hired help at the parties they hosted. Holding company dinners at her own home at least had the immediate benefit of making her the de facto alpha female.

She had just poured a second round of drinks when Inday ushered in a latecomer. The men automatically sat up and drained their glasses, practically smacking their lips at the surprise amuse bouche that stood before them now in stiletto heels. The partners' wives scrutinized the newcomer for far different reasons, looking with envy and trepidation at the sleek honey-skinned figure, which appeared to have been poured into a black bodycon dress then garnished with pearls. She was at least 15 years younger and as many pounds slimmer than the other women.

That made it impossible to like her.

"Socorro I hope you don't mind, we invited a colleague who's visiting from head office." Miguel Punzalan raised his glass in a toast to the new arrival. "This is Cassandra Villareal, just in from New York. She and Amado are working on the telecommunications merger this year. We wanted to welcome her with a Filipino feast."

"How nice of you to come," Socorro handed her a drink. "You look too young to be a lawyer—did you grow up in New York?"

"Chicago, actually. My father's a doctor who migrated from Manila in the '60s."

"I knew you were Filipino, Cassandra. I can always tell from the eyes; it's always in the eyes," Bea cooed, stretching out her vowels in her languid Ilongga way. It was clear she planned to peddle her baubles to this expat before the year was out.

"Actually I'm only half Filipino, my mom is Greek-American. That explains the clunky name." Cassandra swirled the glass of sangria with a slender, ring-free hand. "But please, call me Cassie."

"Doesn't Cassandra mean catastrophe in Greek?" Soledad teased.

"Not quite. It means 'She who entangles men," Cassandra replied.

"Consider us warned," Socorro raised her glass at the other wives. "Shall we go in to dinner?"

Bea launched her charm offensive as Inday ladled out the pansit molo. "So Cassandra, how long do you plan to be with us? I hope you won't let these men bore you with work, there's so much to see outside of Manila...."

"Oh, but I enjoy the work—and anyway I'm still getting to know the city. Amado was kind enough to give me a quick tour of the Glorietta at lunch the other day."

"How very kind of him," Soledad raised an eyebrow at Socorro's husband, who was chasing a dumpling around his soup bowl.

*   *   *

By the time Socorro began delivering heart-shaped tortes for Valentine's, Amado's appetite had begun to wane. At first he declined dessert, claiming he had to lose the extra pounds he'd gained over Christmas. Second servings were the next to go. Soon after that he simply stopped coming home for dinner. By March, Inday had stopped asking if her Ate was dining alone and simply set a single plate for Socorro each night.

Amado claimed late nights at the law firm were running him into the ground, and yet he seemed remarkably chipper. Socorro often heard her husband humming Tony Bennett tunes while shaving in the morning. One day she discovered him preening before her full-length mirror, sucking in his gut and craning his neck to diminish the double chin that threatened to engulf his jaw.

"Give it up, Ading," she joked. "Those extra pounds aren't going anywhere. Middle age is upon us."

"Speak for yourself, Socorro." He sprayed cologne on both palms and rubbed his neck. "I'm not ready to enter the golden years just yet."

Amado picked up his briefcase. "Don't wait up. We have a conference call with the head office. I doubt we'll be done before midnight."

Socorro leaned over to steal a kiss but her husband was already reaching for the door. Glancing back, he sighed.

"Really Socorro, maybe you should take Soledad's advice and have some work done. Just because you're middle-aged doesn't mean you have to look it."

And then he was gone.

Socorro avoided looking in the mirror that had earlier lied to Amado. When had her husband turned into Peter Pan? How could he think she had overtaken him in the race to senescence? She took a deep, calming breath.... And why on earth did their bedroom suddenly smell of lavender, sage and rosemary?

She glanced at Amado's dresser and understood. After a decade of Grey Flannel, her stolid husband had switched to something called Egoiste Platinum. By Chanel.

Amado, whose machismo had been nurtured by Jesuits then forged in steel by his fraternity, would not have been caught dead sampling cologne at the Chanel counter, not even in some foreign Duty Free emporium far away from his hidebound peers at the law firm. No, this could only have been purchased by the sort of woman who wanted to smell summer in Provence whenever she nuzzled Amado's no-longer-young neck.

Who could confirm her suspicions, Socorro wondered. The good lawyers at Samson, Punzalan and Santuico would never betray a colleague and pride prevented her from investigating her husband, acting like the stereotypical jealous wife.

It was a pity Amado preferred to drive his own car; a driver could have told her his daily itinerary: where he went for lunch, if he stopped anywhere after work; if a woman had shared the ride. After splurging on a late model Jaguar, Amado felt compelled to drive himself everywhere. The man could barely stand to surrender his trophy car to valet parking.

Socorro decided she needed something more solid than aftershave to prove her husband was cheating. Meanwhile, she strove to maintain a semblance of normality, catering Easter dinners, Mother's day brunches,

and wedding banquets as Manila simmered through the sultry summer
months.

*   *   *

Her patience was rewarded by Amado himself, who had not shed
his habit of clinching deals over meals—in this case, lunch. Socorro was
rushing to meet a client at Glorietta mall that Friday when she spotted
her husband through the glassed-in patio of a bistro. He wasn't dining
alone. Ducking behind an oversized box planter, she proceeded to spy
on Amado and She-Who-Entangles-Men.

Cassandra leaned rather too closely into Amado's shoulder, looking
at him from under her false eyelashes. He must have said something
amusing, for at that moment she giggled, cupped his cheek, and pulled
him into a brief kiss.

Socorro could not bear to see more. She turned hastily and nearly
tripped over a passing stroller. The uniformed yaya pulled it back with a
yelp before Socorro could trample her sleeping ward. Socorro hurried off,
hoping her sunglasses could provide sufficient cover when the dam broke.

*   *   *

Socorro spent some weeks brooding over her situation and gradually
indignation replaced her grief. On the one hand, the marriage as she had
known it had gone rancid. On the other, she now had the trump card
with which to claim the one thing Amado had never given her: a child.

At 40, she was aware that the odds of conception were dismal. Nev-
ertheless, there were hormone cocktails and procedures that could signifi-
cantly improve these odds, cures to infertility that could now be paid for
with the guilt money she intended to extort from her faithless husband.

She laid the groundwork by performing due diligence. She visited
a fertility specialist, had her hormones measured, discussed the results
with her doctor. By the time the typhoon season began, she had all the
evidence she needed to make her case.

*   *   *

The monsoon was intent on drowning Manila that Sunday. The
rain's rhythmic drumming enveloped Socorro's kitchen in a cocoon of
warmth, scented by lamb shanks braising in a pot and herbed potatoes

roasting in the oven. She had given the cook the day off so that she alone could prepare a special meal for the deal she hoped to clinch with Amado.

"Something smells good. Are you catering tonight?" her husband strolled into the kitchen.

"No, actually," Socorro stirred olives into the stew and seasoned the gravy. "I thought we could have a nice Sunday dinner for a change, just the two of us."

"Ay Socorro, I wish you'd told me earlier—the New York office wants some paperwork faxed over, first thing Monday morning," Amado dipped a wooden spoon into the pot and fished out an olive. "That means I'm going to have to go into the office tonight."

He slurped up the olive and chewed noisily. "Mmm... tastes like you've been cooking this all day. Maybe I can take it in for lunch tomorrow?"

Socorro snatched the spoon from him and tossed it into the sink. "When will you stop lying, Amado? You're not really going to the office tonight, are you?"

"I don't know what you mean, Sweetham. Where else would I be going?"

"Maybe I should ask Cassandra."

"What does Cassie have to do with it?"

"What does Cassie have to do with you?"

"If you're implying that—"

"How stupid do you think I am, Ading?" Socorro reached past him and pulled a large chef's knife from its block. "I know all about the two of you."

Keeping an eye on the blade, Amado replied with the coolly impersonal lawyer's voice he used on his most recalcitrant clients. "You don't know a damn thing about—"

"Don't patronize me. I saw you Ading. Kissing her in broad daylight at Café Havana two months ago I saw you." BAM! Socorro slammed the knife broadside against the chopping board with her fist. The garlic clove beneath popped neatly out of its skin.

She took more cloves from a bowl and smacked the knife blade over each one as Amado slowly backed away from the counter.

"I asked Lillia the other day—she said she's known about it for months... just like everyone else at your office knew. You're apparently the last partner to pick up a querida. Pués better late than never, no?" Socorro furiously minced the garlic into a paste.

"Can you blame me? All you think about is food. You create these elaborate feasts for people you barely know, then you help them eat it. Have you looked at yourself lately?" Amado waved at Socorro's stained apron.

Socorro didn't bother to glance down. She was well aware that her body had expanded apace with her catering business. After all, what credibility could a skinny cook claim?

"How dare you make my weight an excuse for cheating! What did you think would happen after all those dinners I catered for your partners, your clients, all those meals for deals? I worked just as hard for your career as you did," Socorro grabbed a fistful of parsley from her herb basket and hacked it into a chiffonade.

"Don't you lay that guilt trip on me—you wanted to host those parties. You said yourself that every event opened the door to more referrals." Amado ran a hand over his thinning hair and glanced out the window. The wind was hurling solid sheets of rain over his Jaguar. "If you think..."

"You obviously don't care what I think," Socorro put down the knife and wiped her hands on her apron. "So let me tell you what I want."

"If you think I'm going to leave Cassie —"

"'Punyeta Amado, I've heard enough about that putatsing. From now on it's going to be all about how you are going to make it up to me."

She pulled a folder out of a kitchen drawer and held it out to him. "There they are, Dr. Ferreira's report, my lab results, the FSH levels, the hormones, everything you need to know about my getting pregnant."

"You can't be pregnant." Amado waved the envelope away.

"Oh, but I intend to be." Socorro stepped forward, jabbing the folder at his chest. "These lab results show I still have a few viable eggs. If we did in vitro..."

"Do you know how much that's going to cost?" Amado slapped the folder out of her hands and scattered its contents on the floor. "At your age, we'll have to do it more than once. Hundreds of thousands of pesos wasted on lousy odds. No, Socorro, we had this discussion ten years ago. I'm not doing it. You can't blackmail me into doing this."

Amado grabbed his keys. "I'm sorry you wasted all this time cooking, but I won't cut any deals off this meal."

As he turned to leave, Socorro reached for the nearest object and flung it at him. The canister shattered against the doorjamb, showering Amado with shards of glass and rock salt.

"Do you really think your hysterics can stop me? Not even this storm could keep me away from her." Amado brushed salt off his shoulders. "Now that everything's out in the open I can stop pretending. I'll sleep in the guest room from now on. Tell Inday to move all my clothes and shoes over there."

"Move them yourself, you bastard!"

But Amado was already sprinting through the rain to his car.

Socorro sank onto a bar stool and stared out the window at their sodden driveway, ignoring the dinner she would have to eat alone.

As Socorro scraped the remains of her dinner into Tupperware, a sports car swerved to overtake a bus along EDSA. It hydroplaned wildly over the flooded freeway then careened into a divider, flipping like an oversized skateboard to land heavily on its roof. The bus driver and his passengers later described how momentum propelled the Jaguar onward several yards until it rammed into a jeep abandoned by the curb.

Shortly after midnight, the new widow was shown into the hospital's morgue. She stood at the head of the table on which the corpse lay hidden beneath a clean white sheet. The female doctor on duty raised the cloth long enough for Socorro to confirm that the deceased was in fact Amado. She closed her eyes briefly and nodded, letting out a slow breath.

"Mrs. Pelaez, I'm so sorry for your loss..." Dra. Benedicto murmured, keeping a respectful distance from the widow. "No one should ever have to see a loved one in this condition. He couldn't possibly have survived that crash, but you know his injuries would have been less severe if he had strapped on his seatbelt."

"No seatbelt? I'm not surprised," Socorro shook her head. "He drives that Jaguar like a crazy teenager. The day he made partner, he went to the dealership and ordered their latest model. 'Liquid Silver'—that's the fancy name the dealership gave the color of his Jaguar."

"It's his favorite toy, you know...I mean, it was his favorite toy," she faltered. "I'm sorry—I really should stop talking as though he were still alive." Socorro absentmindedly patted her husband's sheet-covered head.

Dr. Benedicto jumped at this rare chance for chitchat; it was usually so quiet down at the morgue. "Mrs. Pelaez, you may not remember me but my name is Chona, Bea Santuico's niece? You catered my despedida de soltera last year—perhaps you knew me by Dayao, my maiden name? I married a Benedicto from Bacolod."

Socorro recalled the November dinner, silverware and leaded crystal goblets gleaming beneath the fairy lights that garlanded the estate's acacias.

"Ah yes, your Tita Bea introduced us at her daughter's debut, I remember now, hija." She smiled. "You and your fiancé made such a lovely couple."

Socorro looked beyond Dra. Benedicto to the shrouded figure and her smile faded. "Strange how life changes, no? Last year I cooked a feast for you and your fiancé, and now here you are, showing me my dead husband."

"Naku Mrs. Pelaez, I'm so sorry, this was the wrong time to bring up my wedding, forgive me." Dr. Benedicto touched Socorro's elbow. "Please, if there's anything at all I can do to help ..."

As Socorro stared at the earnest young doctor, the seed of an idea sprouted in her mind. Walking halfway down the table, she lifted the sheet. While most of Amado was barely recognizable, his private parts were in pristine condition. She turned to Dr. Benedicto and framed her request as delicately as possible.

"You know, Amado wanted to be cremated. Pero hija, I loved my husband at least as much as you love yours...and the thought of every last bit of him going up in smoke..." Socorro wiped away an insincere tear. "It's just too much to bear."

Anticipating a storm of weeping, Dra. Benedicto stepped forward to offer her stock phrases of sympathy, but the widow rambled on.

"We were not blessed with children. After the funeral I will have nothing to remind me of him."

"I know this is highly irregular but please hija, could you give me this one small piece of my husband to take home? It's the only part of him that still looks whole..." Socorro raised the sheet high enough for Dra. Benedicto to see Amado's limp penis.

"I just want to bury it in our garden, under his favorite mango tree."

Startled, the doctor drew back but Socorro pressed on, lowering her voice as though afraid that the neighboring dead would overhear.

"Please Chona, do this for your Tita Socorro. The other doctors don't have to find out. It's the middle of the night, the morticians are coming in the morning and I will explain the missing ... portion to them. I promise you won't get into trouble." Socorro grabbed the doctor's hand. "Please indulge this old widow."

"I suppose it's just a simple excision. All right, Tita. Ordinarily I would never do such a thing, but for you..." Chona extricated her hand from Socorro's crushing grip. "Let me find a scalpel —"

*   *   *

Socorro had declared a hiatus from cooking during her period of mourning, but after the ninth day of prayers, she returned to her kitchen with a vengeance.

The day after his cremation, Amado Pelaez's ashes filled a heavy silver urn that claimed its place of honor atop the dining room credenza. The balance of his remains sat on the butcher's block, newly thawed and ready to enrich the entree Socorro was preparing for a special dinner guest.

Socorro sliced the shaft and scrotum into anonymous cubes then stirred them into a thick stew of chicken thighs, pig's feet and mashed black beans. The pot muttered portentously, exhaling breaths redolent with anise and garlic.

It had been relatively easy to summon Cassandra to this intimate dinner. Socorro simply enlisted the aid of the partners' wives, who nagged their husbands into insisting the junior associate attend a despedida dinner before she returned to New York.

So it was that barely two weeks after the tragic accident, the two women sat across from each other, Amado's urn perched just beyond the cabisera.

"You really shouldn't have gone to all this trouble," Cassandra began as Socorro ladled a generous portion of stew onto her guest's plate.

"No trouble at all, dear, cooking is my therapy. Amado always spoke so highly of you and your…" Socorro handed Cassandra her plate, "…work. I know he would have wanted to send you off with a little despedida. Please, try this. It was one of his favorite dishes."

Socorro watched mesmerized as Cassandra speared a cube of flesh and slid the fork into her mouth, chewing with obvious relish.

"No wonder Amado liked this. It's so tender and hmmm, I don't know, savory in a pungent way? I've never tasted anything like it. You really are an amazing cook." She saluted Socorro with her wine glass and took a sip.

Socorro nodded graciously and drank with her. "You know, I was just wondering, when was the last time you saw my husband before the car crash?"

Cassandra swirled the wine in her glass, suddenly mesmerized by its blood red hue. "That would have been on Friday afternoon at the office."

"But wasn't that one of those weekends when you both had to pull extra hours at the firm? There were so many of them…"

"Lord, no. It was raining so hard that Sunday, I refused to leave my condo. We got Chinese take-out for dinner."

"We?" Socorro raised her eyebrows.

Cassandra speared another chunk of meat with her fork. "I had a visitor."

"Anyone I know?" Socorro smiled but her eyes were cold.

Cassandra's fork paused midway to her mouth. "If you don't mind, I'd rather not talk about it. It ended badly." She slipped the fork into her mouth and chewed vigorously.

Socorro picked at her mango salad and patiently watched the younger woman finish her dinner. Bite. Chew. Swallow. Bite. Chew. Swallow.

They ate in awkward silence until, with a discreet burp, Cassandra made a feeble attempt at chitchat.

"So is this a Filipino dish? It doesn't taste anything like adobo."

"It's actually a similar stew called Talunang Manok." Socorro dabbed at her mouth with a napkin. "The tradition among cockfighters is, after a rooster is killed, he isn't simply tossed into the trash bin. The sabungero takes him home and cooks him for dinner that night. We Filipinos hate to see anything go to waste."

Socorro folded her napkin, carefully smoothing the wrinkles around Amado's monogrammed initials. "In other words Cassandra, what you are eating is the defeated cock...he lost, you see."

Cassie looked momentarily confused. "I could have sworn I was eating pork just now."

Socorro gazed at her dead husband's lover with unexpected pity. "You're right, of course. He really was a pig."

"Frida Kahlo Reincarnated as a Lion" by David Sheskin

THREE POEMS
by Samm Genessee

< so shut your eyes against my kiss >

yesterday a dictator rose bloomed in the countryside, stereo playing funk
and the old man's hubba hubba

but what do you know about past lives // let me be honest into your eyes
like a lake along the road showing you earth's single meaning

I'm your sister and I have been to all the places people go to know
so shut your eyes against my kiss and let company be your salvation

round hay bales, army guys eating breakfast // nothing shocks a witch
nothing contains the view unless I do, and I can do more than silence can

fire's in your heart too much, so grab my sleepy corridor
and get yourself my love

< sex goblet>
[enshrining myself]

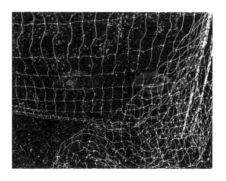

wherever I look there's another island [flying]
skin keys into me, push me over / into the sound
the maiden snaps + is gone

key into me myself, darkly reconcile
green after a singe / the chorus
feed us to each other
love is a long way through

wanting good times in a ghost town
wherever i look / pleated, galactic // two faces
doubling my own
+ even then, distilling the world's sap drip by
drip by hand by taste, firing earth into one

a fool called this "the house of honey" // Mudhushala
is the house of wine // shahad ka ghar
lip to lip the dream goes and is swallowed
loveliness takes off what she doesn't need

now I am able to meet you, now my thirsting soul

pulls out a darkness, + in its command
what predictably there always is, a willingness
the forest where we live

༄༅༚

\<féminine histoire\>

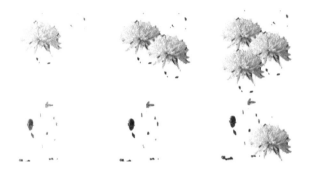

if a man is there when I close my eyes // birds feast
if you forget, how do you know if you can if you want? // 2 red roses
or else see, I see, the inmost kernel of the lilac's buttery light

when I close my eyes, Joanna appears smoking a menthol in a nightshirt, long black hair
Spanish way with English, tells of dancing with a married 30 yr. old who plays trumpet
in a 12-man band in Southgate

for me, that sharp edge gets wild // clouds roll over the moon // I'd never seen a storm like that
and now the féminine histoire pulls me in deep // lotus flowers, lily pads, dusk and fresh fruit // it
makes sense to assume // ticonderoga // melting the stormiest of hearts

༄༅༚

ALT TEXT FOR 10
NON-EXISTENT PHOTOS
by Rahne Alexander

GOLF CART

This is me and Donna Kaz and Chimimanda Adichie, riding together in a golf cart at the Baltimore Book Festival. We're not posing, we're just off for a ride down the main corridor of booksellers and food booths. The sun is high in the clear blue sky over the busy festival wrapped around the concourse of Baltimore's Inner Harbor. A crisp picturesque autumn. Donna Kaz has just published her memoir, and I'm about to do a public conversation with her about the book, which taught me a lot—particularly about what a prick William Hurt was, and that's given me complicated feelings about one of my favorite Chantal Akerman films. Donna is amazing, and we've since become friends. I go up and teach at her writing conferences every so often. One of these days, she and I will do a country duet together. I'd read some of the unkind things Chimimanda wrote and said about trans women and, as a result, have kept an arm's length from her works. She gets the front seat next to the driver; me and Donna want to ride together in the back anyway, so everybody's happy. The whole ride I keep hoping some phone snaps a photo. Imagine my delight when I found it on Instagram.

BREAKFAST FOR DINNER

This one is a funny one; it's just me, flat on my back. I'm still in my diner apron and polo shirt, and if you look closely, you can see there are eggs and sausage and potatoes and coffee all over the place. There's the styrofoam containers. It almost never snows or ices over in Santa Cruz, but this year it sure did. I'd never experienced ice on the house steps before; I had no idea what I was walking into. My graveyard shift was over, and I was bringing home my dinner, a breakfast combo #4, which I would share with Colette, my cat. Colette especially loved the #4. Now our dinner was all over the ground. I'd never fallen so fast in my life. I'm not really hurt—I've fortunately always been pretty good at falling—but right there I'm wondering what I'm going to do about dinner. I'm wondering what I'm going to say to Colette.

RIBTICKLER

I'm not ready to write about Asshole yet, but when I do I'll begin with this photo of me with a newly broken rib in the airport in Puerto Vallarta, carrying my suitcase-without-wheels. Asshole and her mom are not in frame, they're up ahead there somewhere. We were on our way out of the country when I stumbled on a short step at the resort hotel and cracked my left rib cage on some decorative garden rocks. I was incredibly drunk on the numerous tequila shots we had been plied with at the restaurant, which seemed all too eager to comp tequila to blonde girls. I was carrying our leftovers then, too, and I was heading to sit by the pool while they freshened up in the lavatory, and whoops, disaster, leftovers and luggage everywhere, the worst pain ever, and all I could think about is how I just lost my stupid dot com job and the health insurance with it—and how hard it is for a trans woman without a cosigner to get insurance at all—and how I had no idea about how medical personnel in Puerto Vallarta would treat a pre-op trans woman who had maybe just broken her rib three hours before getting on a plane home, which was where I lived with Asshole. The hotel manager said there was no medic on staff on Sundays, that he could call the Red Cross for me if I wanted. I was in a great deal of pain, but I had just squandered all of my severance money on this dumb trip and could not risk missing the plane if I could help it. Asshole initially reacted like I was faking it, as usual. She always treated me as if I were a phony, and I had finally come to resent it. I stood up

and rinsed my head by the pool, wondering if I had punctured a lung
maybe and what would happen to someone with a punctured lung on
an airplane. I dried off and realized that my poor-girl suitcase didn't have
wheels. Asshole didn't offer to help me, and I wasn't about to debase
myself and beg her. So I carried my own baggage home.

SYNCOPE

This one is sort of a photograph within a photograph, another where I'm
flat on my back, and you're seeing my perspective. There's my best friend,
Melissa, and Mr. Davis and Michelle Hernandez and Michelle S. Hernandez, they're all peering down at me, and they all look two-dimensional,
like they're a photograph. A photograph within a photograph. This was
the time I fainted in senior year civics class. It was a class everyone had
to take, so it was kind of an equalizer class. I was mostly bored out of
my mind and impatient with the members of my cohort who couldn't
complete a blank map of the 50 states. I was at the peak of my eating
disorder, totally in control of everything. I usually ate a single piece of
buttered toast in the morning, a Dr. Pepper and a 3 Musketeers for brunch
at school, and then in the evening we'd have family dinner, a casserole
maybe. This was an unusually warm February Friday and the teacher, who
made no secret of his evangelical side, was given to sharing assorted life
advice after he ran out of civics things to teach. That day he was talking
about recognizing symptoms of various ailments, and he had just started
talking about epilepsy when I lost consciousness. My face slammed down
on my desk and my lip split open, and then I rolled out of my chair and
flopped out on my back on the floor. Mr. Davis lifted me up to my desk,
worried that he had somehow summoned a seizure by talking about epilepsy, and said, "Don't you want to go to the nurse?" I declined and said
I'm fine, I just didn't eat today, which was true. I said I needed to sit for
a while before I moved anyway, so let's just keep class going, and if I feel
like I need to see the nurse, I'll go. And of course I didn't; instead I went
home and learned the word "syncope" from *Taber's Medical Encyclope-
dia*, the same manual that helped me diagnose my own transsexuality.
On Monday, Mr. Davis found out that I didn't see the nurse, and that

this faggot who was otherwise a stellar student and never had a blemish on her record was suddenly passing out in class in her last semester of high school, so well maybe that's something to call the parents about he thought, so he called and told my dad. When I got home from school on Monday I was grilled by my father about doing drugs. I swore that I was not doing drugs, but I'm not entirely sure he believed me because he said at the end of the scolding that he wasn't going to tell my mother about how I passed out in class. I never asked him to do that. I don't know if he ever told my mother.

CLIFFHANGER

There was this one professor at Santa Cruz who, I was told, had a complaint file thick with sexist behavior. During one class, he apparently told my friend A that women were incapable of great writing. I always wanted to see what this piece of shit looked like, and here he was at the poetry reading on campus. A pointed him out and he looked more or less like I thought he would. I said to A, what if I stuck my foot out in the aisle as he's walking down the college classroom stairs and trip him, and we laughed, but then I realized, as you can see from the photograph, that's Adrienne Rich and Michelle Cliff chatting at the bottom of the stairs near the podium and it wouldn't be a good look for a tranny like me to send an agent of the patriarchy bowling over two of the most iconic living lesbian poets. So I pulled my foot back under my seat and whatshisname walked free.

JANE ROE

Here I am with Norma McCorvey and Gloria Allred when they came to Redlands, the land o' the reds, and spoke in the campus chapel. Norma had just come out as Jane Roe, after years of relative anonymity, and was now on the college circuit. I had just come to the understanding that I had got some emotional work to do before I could go out to clinic defenses again because my anger burns too hot. Still, look, I'm thrilled to meet this hero of body autonomy. I am 100% clear that my own relationship to my body is a reproductive rights issue. Norma's fight is my fight. Just a few years later the evangelicals got to her. The news broke my heart, and for a while I kept a newspaper clipping of her conversion story pinned to the fabric of my cubicle wall at Papier-Maché Press. What they must have thought of me, this brash young transsexual bus rider who wore drapey turtlenecks in California, lamenting the loss of Norma McCorvey in the most important battle of the 20th century. I guess one of the morals of this story is that visibility may be a net positive, but for a lot of us, that net is really also a trap. Years later, a young filmmaker I considered a friend, who was slipping from Bernie fervor and into Trump allegiance, issued his online dismay that I was likely about to vote for Hillary Clinton and wanted me to explain myself. I told him that I thought it was crucial to put Hillary in office to provide protection for Roe v. Wade, that there was no more important issue. He responded with the puzzling statement that Hillary had "ruined feminism" for him, at least in part because she did not abandon Bill Clinton upon the revelation of his infidelity. I responded, if that's your definition of feminist betrayal, I somehow doubt your commitment to Sparkle Motion. If I've learned one thing in this line of work, it's that if you can't handle betrayal, the project of liberation is probably not for you.

WONDER WOMAN

The Commish and I got tickets to this political event celebrating Maryland Women in Politics because we were both working for the Creative Alliance, which was one of Barbara Mikulski's favorite projects. No one else from the org was able to go, so we got dressed up and went to hang out with fancy people in the DC suburbs. It was every woman in Maryland Democratic politics and then some. Lynda Carter was the guest of honor, and Madeleine Albright, and Barbara Mikulski, too. I was new to town so I didn't recognize many of the lesser electeds. I'd decided to wear these insane four-inch Tom Ford pumps I'd gotten on a lark at one of those discount designer pop up shops that Jordan and Robert dragged me to in my first year in Baltimore. These pumps were the only shoes I brought with me, and there was only one chair in the room and that belonged to Lynda Carter, who was gorgeous and friendly, and if I wasn't in tremendous pain from the shoes, I might have tried to introduce myself. Instead, this is me idly nursing a cocktail and leaning against a silver-colored high top table and waiting for The Commish to come back and tell me if she was able to find out how much Madeline Albright could bench press.

ZOE

Zoe is one of the only trans women in Santa Cruz who seemed to want to talk to me as a peer. I'd mostly only see her on the bus with her large glasses and her long hippie hair. I was inexplicably in this wireless rims phase, and my hair was a L'oreal Paris Black mop, and we were on one of those buses to Scotts Valley with the seats that face each other, which ordinarily were a nightmare but quite pleasant when you had a friend to chat with and create a more insulated space. Any third party was going to have to sit next to two trans femmes vibing, the most terrifying energy in the world. We lost touch and she died a few years back, but she briefly appears in this documentary about Robert Anton Wilson called *Maybe Logic*. I understand that he is very popular. I bought a copy on DVD so I could still see her sometimes.

MOM, ME

Mom and I are sitting side by side on her hospital bed. I'm wearing my forest green A-line dress, which fits me like a glove; the first dress I ever got trapped in while still in the dressing room of the vintage shop. She's wearing a dressing gown and her full smile, the one she passed to me, hamming for the camera. Her hair is so lush, I don't know how she does it. Mine is self-cut into a shapeless flyaway bob. She's just told me that she's finally going to teach me to cut my hair like she should have years ago. We have a laugh about that, and I help her into her chair and take her out to the front room so we can look at her roses outside her beloved picture windows.

BYSTANDER

This is an Instagram shot from some random bystander. The photo shows my left side, and I am on all fours, extended child pose. My belly is distended, and I am clearly in considerable distress. My New Pornographers t-shirt is torn and my skirt is at my knees. Nobody can figure out what's going on, they're all standing around. Look at that one woman, she looks like Ruth Buzzi. I cannot tell you how important Ruth Buzzi was for me. Ruth Buzzi doesn't know what to do. She can't believe her eyes. She's watching this awkward woman just fall down in the street and... give birth? To...something? I honestly don't remember any of this happening at all. I remember just walking down the street, and suddenly everything went grey and next thing I know, I'm throwing up in an ambulance. They kept me for observation for a couple of days and never figured out what happened, so they let me out, but not before the attending physician reminded me again to lose some weight. I'm still paying off that bill.

"Anne Frank Reincarnated as a Lion Proteecting the Oppressed"
by David Sheskin

A RESPECTABLE WOMAN
by Kate Chopin

Mrs. Baroda was a little provoked to learn that her husband expected his friend, Gouvernail, up to spend a week or two on the plantation.

They had entertained a good deal during the winter; much of the time had also been passed in New Orleans in various forms of mild dissipation. She was looking forward to a period of unbroken rest, now, and undisturbed tête-a-tête with her husband, when he informed her that Gouvernail was coming up to stay a week or two.

This was a man she had heard much of but never seen. He had been her husband's college friend; was now a journalist, and in no sense a society man or "a man about town," which were, perhaps, some of the reasons she had never met him. But she had unconsciously formed an image of him in her mind. She pictured him tall, slim, cynical; with eye-glasses, and his hands in his pockets; and she did not like him. Gouvernail was slim enough, but he wasn't very tall nor very cynical; neither did he wear eye-glasses nor carry his hands in his pockets. And she rather liked him when he first presented himself.

But why she liked him she could not explain satisfactorily to herself when she partly attempted to do so. She could discover in him none of those brilliant and promising traits which Gaston, her husband, had often assured her that he possessed. On the contrary, he sat rather mute and receptive before her chatty eagerness to make him feel at home and in face of Gaston's frank and wordy hospitality. His manner was as courteous toward her as the most exacting woman could require; but he made no direct appeal to her approval or even esteem.

Once settled at the plantation he seemed to like to sit upon the wide portico in the shade of one of the big Corinthian pillars, smoking his cigar lazily and listening attentively to Gaston's experience as a sugar planter.

"This is what I call living," he would utter with deep satisfaction, as
the air that swept across the sugar field caressed him with its warm and
scented velvety touch. It pleased him also to get on familiar terms with
the big dogs that came about him, rubbing themselves sociably against
his legs. He did not care to fish, and displayed no eagerness to go out and
kill grosbecs when Gaston proposed doing so.

Gouvernail's personality puzzled Mrs. Baroda, but she liked him.
Indeed, he was a lovable, inoffensive fellow. After a few days, when she
could understand him no better than at first, she gave over being puzzled
and remained piqued. In this mood she left her husband and her guest,
for the most part, alone together. Then finding that Gouvernail took no
manner of exception to her action, she imposed her society upon him,
accompanying him in his idle strolls to the mill and walks along the
batture. She persistently sought to penetrate the reserve in which he had
unconsciously enveloped himself.

"When is he going—your friend?" she one day asked her husband.
"For my part, he tires me frightfully."

"Not for a week yet, dear. I can't understand; he gives you no trouble."

"No. I should like him better if he did; if he were more like others,
and I had to plan somewhat for his comfort and enjoyment."

Gaston took his wife's pretty face between his hands and looked
tenderly and laughingly into her troubled eyes. They were making a bit
of toilet sociably together in Mrs. Baroda's dressing-room.

"You are full of surprises, ma belle," he said to her. "Even I can never
count upon how you are going to act under given conditions." He kissed
her and turned to fasten his cravat before the mirror.

"Here you are," he went on, "taking poor Gouvernail seriously and
making a commotion over him, the last thing he would desire or expect."

"Commotion!" she hotly resented. "Nonsense! How can you say
such a thing?

Commotion, indeed! But, you know, you said he was clever."

So he is. But the poor fellow is run down by overwork now. That's
why I asked him here to take a rest."

"You used to say he was a man of ideas," she retorted, unconciliated.

"I expected him to be interesting, at least. I'm going to the city in the morning to have my spring gowns fitted. Let me know when Mr. Gouvernail is gone; I shall be at my Aunt Octavie's."

That night she went and sat alone upon a bench that stood beneath a live oak tree at the edge of the gravel walk.

She had never known her thoughts or her intentions to be so confused. She could gather nothing from them but the feeling of a distinct necessity to quit her home in the morning.

Mrs. Baroda heard footsteps crunching the gravel; but could discern in the darkness only the approaching red point of a lighted cigar. She knew it was Gouvernail, for her husband did not smoke. She hoped to remain unnoticed, but her white gown revealed her to him. He threw away his cigar and seated himself upon the bench beside her; without a suspicion that she might object to his presence.

"Your husband told me to bring this to you, Mrs. Baroda," he said, handing her a filmy, white scarf with which she sometimes enveloped her head and shoulders. She accepted the scarf from him with a murmur of thanks, and let it lie in her lap.

He made some commonplace observation upon the baneful effect of the night air at that season. Then as his gaze reached out into the darkness, he murmured, half to himself:

" 'Night of south winds—night of the large few stars!
   Still nodding night—' "

She made no reply to this apostrophe to the night, which indeed, was not addressed to her.

Gouvernail was in no sense a diffident man, for he was not a self-conscious one. His periods of reserve were not constitutional, but the result of moods. Sitting there beside Mrs. Baroda, his silence melted for the time.

He talked freely and intimately in a low, hesitating drawl that was not unpleasant to hear. He talked of the old college days when he and Gaston had been a good deal to each other; of the days of keen and blind ambitions and large intentions. Now there was left with him, at least, a philosophic acquiescence to the existing order—only a desire to be permitted to exist, with now and then a little whiff of genuine life, such as he was breathing now.

Her mind only vaguely grasped what he was saying. Her physical being was for the moment predominant. She was not thinking of his words, only drinking in the tones of his voice. She wanted to reach out her hand in the darkness and touch him with the sensitive tips of her fingers upon the face or the lips. She wanted to draw close to him and whisper against his cheek—she did not care what—as she might have done if she had not been a respectable woman.

The stronger the impulse grew to bring herself near him, the further, in fact, did she draw away from him. As soon as she could do so without an appearance of too great rudeness, she rose and left him there alone.

Before she reached the house, Gouvernail had lighted a fresh cigar and ended his apostrophe to the night.

Mrs. Baroda was greatly tempted that night to tell her husband—who was also her friend—of this folly that had seized her. But she did not yield to the temptation. Beside being a respectable woman she was a very sensible one; and she knew there are some battles in life which a human being must fight alone.

When Gaston arose in the morning, his wife had already departed. She had taken an early morning train to the city. She did not return till Gouvernail was gone from under her roof.

There was some talk of having him back during the summer that followed. That is, Gaston greatly desired it; but this desire yielded to his wife's strenuous opposition.

However, before the year ended, she proposed, wholly from herself, to have Gouvernail visit them again. Her husband was surprised and delighted with the suggestion coming from her.

"I am glad, chère amie, to know that you have finally overcome your dislike for him; truly he did not deserve it."

"Oh," she told him, laughingly, after pressing a long, tender kiss upon his lips, "I have overcome everything! You will see. This time I shall be very nice to him."

TWO POEMS
by Kathryn deLancellotti

American Girl in Italy, 1951
After Kim Addonizio's "What Do Women Want?"

The photo hung above our toilet
in a golden frame.

She seemed to move in slow motion
across the old stone sidewalk,

clutching her shawl, trying to pass
the corner café, leave behind

fifteen sets of eyes.
Even then I understood

her quickening pulse,
the man on the motorbike

checking out her ass, the shameless
one grabbing his crotch.

I've walked that ancient street,
in that black dress

to open mouths spitting red

wine, past tongues

whistling, truck drivers
flashing porno mags.

The photo confirmed my place—
those strappy sandals,

that dark street,
all those eyes I wear

like bones, like skin
I pull from its hanger, unzip.

୧ඁ◉ඁ

Oval Window

I saw a red-bellied finch
with strands of auburn hair in its beak,
watched it tangle dead cells into nest, wildly
weave me into home. My reflection captured
in stained glass—

saw Mother living in my skin, heard Father
say my face could take me places,
noticed the way eyes never age.

I filled a bath, left a bowl of seed.
The bird hovered then flew away.

> I thought of Sacred Heart Elementary—
> how we were taught to pray for a husband.
> How the kids laughed at the pretty girl
> the day her canary died during show and tell.
> No one felt bad for her.
> We were taught to pity the girl with leg braces; told
> she doesn't stand a chance without a man.

I watched the mother bird dive
towards an approaching male.

❧❧❧

CONCEPCIÓN
by Galel A. Medina

The dark and quiet of the early morning filled her lungs when Eva took her first breath outside her cabin. It had rained just a few hours ago, and the chill that blushed her cheeks comforted her. She built her usual fire and took great pleasure in the crackling of the wood, the scent of the burning pine. Her mother had not left her much, but she had at least instilled in her the appreciation for the solitude of a cheesemaker's work.

Nicolás laid asleep in his wicker chair with his jeans unbuttoned and his mouth open. The mines kept him late—he never made it past that armchair. *Ay mujer, my joints hurt. They work me like a donkey, and you can't even be bothered to fix me a plate with some meat? Don't I make enough to afford more than a pound of beans?* Eva knew better than to talk back; her husband had a way about him. Like a tusa she used to light her fires, he would burn bright and furious, only to be extinguished in the next breath. She was thankful for the work that kept her busy, for the calluses on her feet that kept her standing. Every curse, she turned into a blessing. Nicolás refused to haul gas up their hill, so she cooked surrounded by mist.

Eva used her mother's same old brick stove and worked under the shabby roof she had built herself. In a small notepad, she kept her orders for the day in the cursive she had learned in the first grade. Three pounds of cuajada for Marta Guitierrez, five pounds for Doña Albania, another five for Julissa—the girl who sold everything and anything by the side of the road. Discovering small wounds on her hands as she squeezed lime juice into a pot made her feel clean, beginning the day with a good burning wash. It was an honest and fine way to live, stoking flames at her cabin on a hill where she could watch the dirt road for the pick-ups and donkeys that made the trip up to her neighborhood.

It came then. When she watched the road for Don Beto's milk mule, when the morning sky became red as if heaven had caught fire. Eva thought she was dreaming, having a nightmare about the apocalypse priests had warned her about so many times. She was sure of it when she saw the burning flame hurling towards the mountains. It fell with such strength that she thought the rock might break and bury the town. She might have said a prayer, had she remembered one. Instead, Eva stood there and waited for the hounds of hell and every other cursed thing to tear her apart.

But none came.

The red faded away into purple, the purple to the deep blue of the madrugada. Eva braved a first step down the steps in her yard. Then a second and a trembling third. She kept her slow pace until she found herself on the dirt road, accepting liters of fresh milk. Don Beto was silent, counting the single bills to give her change. His mustache twitched, and his nose breathed back the snot from the chill, as if hell had not been real a minute ago.

"Did you see it, Don Beto?" She asked, with one hand curled around her apron.

"See what?" He scratched under his straw hat, his gray hair already damp from the day's work.

"The sky!" Eva raised her voice and felt a shudder. "It cracked *open*! Clouds as dark as the blood in my veins!"

"Uy," He eyed her with suspicion but did not seem too perturbed. "Seems like the Devil's returned to Concepción. You watch out, Evita. If he's back, he is looking to make a deal. Satanás is a greedy son of a bitch."

She stood there not knowing what to say to his words. He spoke as if this was just a brigand that had returned to town demanding the local tavern serve him the best rum. Not Evil itself. He tied a rubber band around the multi-colored bills he carried and pocketed them.

"Aren't you concerned? Shouldn't we be going to the Mayor? Or the Church?" Anxiety brewed deep within her bowels.

"Don't worry too much about these things, Evita," He smiled and tipped his hat the way fathers always did when they wanted their daughters to stop talking. "He'll collect a soul or two and be on his way. Just make sure that one of them isn't yours. Don't you go looking for him."

"Why would I?"

Don Beto gave her a knowing look before clicking his tongue and pulling his mule along the dirt path.

The Devil became the talk of the town. Rumors floated around on just who had gone to see him and why. Don Luis Orozco had made the journey to the Devil's mountain to ask for twenty heads of cattle; it was of everyone's opinion that he should have at least asked for sixty for such a steep price. Doña Julia Pineda had sold her soul to him, according to the verduleras on the market, for a new house with ceramic floors. Poor woman, they said, if she had just held on until election time, that house would have only cost her a vote in the ballot box.

"Bah," Eva's sister, Geraldina, fanned herself in their secluded corner at a neighbor's sixty-sixth birthday party. They claimed she had gotten the roasted lamb courtesy of the Morning Star. "It's all bullshit if you ask me. Montón de envidiosos, they cannot account for someone else's success without invoking the Devil."

"If it's not the Devil, then what was that thing?" Eva said over the sweet, wooden sound of the marimba.

"I don't know, I'm no scientist, or priest." Geraldina waved at someone across the room. "But why would Satanás promise so little? Makes no sense."

Her words gave Eva pause, she had not stopped thinking about Don Beto's warnings, his assuredness that Eva could be one of those that would seek him out. The old man had looked at Eva like she knew her sister's secrets and the whispers inside her house.

"Oh my God," Her sister nudged at her ribs. "*What* is your bull of a husband doing?"

Panic washed over Eva like a torrent of cold water. She didn't have to guess, to look, to know shame. Still, when he slipped that ring on her finger, she knew Nicolás had become her problem. Her responsibility. There he was, with his shirt half buttoned and slurring his way through an argument. Not everyone understood that his bursts would soon die down, some mistook his feeble sparks for fire. Some took him seriously, not for a rooster puffing his chest.

"Mujer!" Nicolás shouted for her, made clumsy gestures to bring her to his side. "Evita, come tell this cerote about that piece of land your daddy left you! Come! Don't make a liar out of me!"

Every head was turned his way, then every stare found her. Grimaces, uncomfortable smiles. The hushed whispers of best friends, who were so glad they never got too close to Eva. The echo of men's laughter reverberated between her ears, the red glow of their cigarettes might as well have burned her. Most of her shame had been kept private, washed as she scrubbed stains away with stones. This moment, it was like a whip had snapped and slashed her.

"Sometimes I wish someone would knock him out cold," Eva breathed out, the confession coming from deep within herself. She leaned against the cool, lime-cured wall, fearing she would fall otherwise. "Sometimes I wish a horse would kick him in the head. Sometimes I wish the mountain would fall on him."

Geraldina eyed her curiously. Though she was younger, the sister she had practically raised, she was taller by a head. It gave her some sort of authority over Eva. Her expression lied between pity and love. A hateful habit she had picked up from city folk she surrounded herself with.

"With your luck, Evita?" She laughed with her whole belly. "You'll need to make the unholiest deal for that. Not even the Devil wants that man."

There were no words to describe the ire she felt as Geraldina helped her settle Nicolás in the back of the only moto-taxi in town. How Tito, the boy who had just turned eighteen and barely had three hairs on his chin, awkwardly helped move his legs to make room for Eva. Her sister said nothing about it, only kissed her cheek and told her she would come by before returning to the capital. Like an obligation, Eva had become that pitiful figure her family visited with a bag of a city grocer and did not think about too often. All by the age of thirty-one, trapped between the cinderblocks of her small house. Her small life.

The bitterness of Nicolás's stench made the inside of her mouth taste rancid, took over the whole sitting room. The smell traveled down her throat and covered her stomach walls with acid. In the first years of their marriage, Eva would take the time to remove his boots, wash his face, and plead with him to please sleep on his side. Maybe she had held out hope that he would change, grow into that responsible man he promised to be when he'd asked to marry her. One day, she had believed, her husband would grant that dream he'd conjured up for her. In the future, he would build her a ranch where she could spend her days surrounded by animals, want for nothing.

Instead Nicolás was greedy with his money, sparing her a small allowance for their expenses. Whatever she made from squeezing whey through cotton she hid from him. In clay pots, in the bank, in old aprons he would never touch. Eva watched drool spill from the corner of his mouth, his head lolled to the side. Like all the drunks every doñita in town judged through narrowed eyes. God forgive her, but in that moment, Eva realized that her indifference had turned into an aged hatred. If she had to explain it, if she wanted to rationalize it, she would have said it was the Devil who got in her and made her seek out the fire that had rained from the heavens. Before she could understand it, before she could stop herself, Eva slipped on her rubber boots and set out in the direction of that infernal comet.

It was late in the night; the people of Concepción did not stay awake long after a party was over. She would have to be quiet, cut her way through the freshly rained ground. The pine needles would muffle her steps, and the river would keep men away from her since they would confuse her with La Sucia, ready to take their sanity and manhood from them. The briskness of the air carried Eva through the sloping terrain, kept her from looking back. Eva was going to make a deal, and she did not know what would come later, but she knew, felt it in the marrow of her bones, that it would be better than bashing stones against Nicolás's piss stained underwear.

With a heaving chest, she arrived at the site where the Devil surely rested. Eva's entire body ached. Maybe being this close to hell gave her a fever, made every muscle tender and willing to do anything to rid her of the pain. The crater was shallow, almost ordinary.

She expected a horned Devil, a serpent that would whisper in her ear. There was nothing, nothing but mud. Geraldina was right; it was all bullshit. Every story was a lie told by green-eyed gossips.

"Can I help you?" A soft voice asked.

Eva took a deep breath and turned around. She was struck then, in a way she never had been. There stood a woman with a mane of curls and bare feet. White and blue cotton was draped over her body; it hung loose over the curve of her hips. Her skin was the color of copper. She could have been carved out from the finest clay in the land. Only a potter's hand could explain the strong lines of her features. Eva's mouth watered with something new and unfamiliar, attraction to a stranger. Eva would have called it sinful, but how could sin make her feel so alive,eel as natural as the breeze running through the woods?

"I —" Eva began, remembering what she had set out to do. "I came to make a deal."

"Ah," The woman said. "You're the first."

"What? That can't be!"

It couldn't be. The Devil had come to Concepción before, He must have. *She* must have. Why else would the old women in town shut their blinds at night? What would men have to fear in the streets? Who else would have brought prosperity to the little town everyone forgot?

"You seem surprised," She pointed out. "I've watched many make their way here, only to turn on their heels and run back the way they came."

"People in town said they had made a deal with Satanás, sold their souls in exchange for a wish." Eva explained as the woman walked past her.

"Is that who you think I am?" She motioned for Eva to follow. "Your adversary?"

No, Eva wanted to say. But she did not have an answer for who this woman could be, this woman who fell from the sky like a star.

"Take off your boots." She pointed at the cheap rubber Eva wore on her feet. "You're disturbing the land."

Eva did as she was told, relished the earth that got between her toes. Devil or not, she felt a compulsion to give this woman everything she wanted. Anything and everything she asked of her. She followed her deeper into the woods, past overgrown roots and the eyes of owls.

"You wanted to make a deal," The woman said, as she tied a length of twine around one of her fingers. "What is it that you want?"

In truth, the anger that brought Eva here had dissipated. She had all but forgotten about Nicolás, and the red-hot humiliation she'd felt. The woman's chiseled profile had cast a spell on her. "Your name, so I do not offend you?" Eva said.

The brazen smirk on the woman's lips should have frightened her, the amber glow of her irises should have pushed Eva to run. "You came unprepared," The woman's voice remained cool, even as her fingers reached for a strand of Eva's hair. "Come back tomorrow with an offering, and if it pleases me, I'll give you my name."

Eva puzzled over the woman's nature in the sleepy quiet of Concepción. Angel, demon. Devil, goddess. She knew next to nothing about the Divine. Pouring warm water over herself in the bath she went over what she, in her smallness, could gift such a being. There was no gold or silver hidden in the mines in Concepción, just metals that could bend and form the skeletons of faraway skyscrapers. The bills she'd kept hidden would be too little, too vulgar. There was only one thing worth anything— the work of her hands. The very best she had ever done—rich and too decadent to be served on a breakfast plate.

Doña Consuelo down the road kept goats for her grandchildren, with some persuading Eva could convince her to let her have some of their milk.

She set out early, that always impressed old women. Doña Consuelo easily agreed to spare the milk, if Eva could share half of what she made with her. No doubt it would be expensive, the woman told her. *And you won't be selling it? Ay mamita, you have to start thinking about working harder. Do you always want to live in that shack?* Eva bit her tongue and chewed on her pride. The old woman had done well for herself, and she saw it fit to remind everyone that they had not. Eva graciously accepted the milk and left with a knot in her throat.

Her determined hands worked at digging the garden for garlic and scallions, pulling fresh rosemary, and cutting them all so finely they could have been beaded onto a tapestry. If there was some sort of magic involved in the deal she had made, then it could be paid with the scent of the herbs and spices alone. Eva thought she might bake her mother's old bread recipe, fire roasted with a hard crust. Some wild berries could be squashed and presented together. She could not be faulted for not doing enough, for not sacrificing the sweat on her brow.

"What are you doing?" Nicolás said, buckling his pants as he stepped outside. "What's all this?"

In her haze, Eva had forgotten the hour and day it was. Sunday, when Nicolás slept late and lingered. She took a deep breath and felt sick at the sight of him. His figure and stench had only fermented overnight.

"I thought I would try something different, is all." She became aware of the demureness of her voice. It was like a bad itch in her throat, one she couldn't cough out.

He scrunched up his nose as he examined her. The wetness of her hands, her covered hair. The apron tied around her waist. Perhaps when the Priest had declared them man and wife, he had given him the right to be repulsed by Eva.

"Where's my breakfast?" Nicolás cocked his head to the side. "Tell me you didn't do *this* instead of frying my eggs and palming my tortillas."

"Of course not," Eva suddenly remembered why she had set out to find the Devil last night, her husband, the proverbial cross upon her shoulders. "Give me a minute to wash up and I'll set the table."

Sunday slothed its way to dusk along with Nicolás. The Sun barely moved in the sky, like some curse had been cast on her. When the blue of the sky became tinted with orange, her pulse began to race. Every beat dropped in anticipation of her husband putting on his hat and not even bothering to lie as he left on some unnamed engagement. Just as soon as he had been lost around the curve, she set out on the path that would take her back to the crater. Past the river and shielded by the woods, Eva did not feel her breathing growing shorter or the burn in her calves, but that familiar heat enveloped her as the site grew closer.

"You came back," This time the woman had been sitting on a boulder, like she had been keeping watch on the road. There was a hint of surprise in her tone, and it pulled at some forgotten tenderness. "And not empty-handed, I see."

"Yes, a deal is a deal," She heard the shyness, but it came with a pleasant flush on her cheeks. "It's not much but I hope it's enough,"

"Don't do that." The woman told her as she slipped off from the boulder and took the small package of bread and cheese from Eva's hands.

"Do what?"

"Speak of yourself like that," Her eyes darkened as she hungrily tore the bread and cheese. She had the look of someone who had forgotten they'd been starving. "It devalues your offering. You wouldn't want that, would you?"

"No." Eva replied simply. It was about all she could do as she took in the sight of full slips savoring her food. Consuming the moans that emanated from her throat.

"My name is Lilit," she said, wiping the crumbs off her lips. "Now, is there something else you want from me?"

Her mind was devoid of anything to do with her husband. Free of the resentment and wrath, the only thought she knew was Lilit. How, now that she could keep her name under her tongue, the night seemed to begin at the tips of her curls.

"Tell me who you are," Eva told her, daring to touch her wrist. Her skin was so soft and cold that it made her gasp in surprise. "I want to learn more about you."

"Aren't you a curious one?" Lilit inspected her. Her bare feet, her covered hair. The wool sweater that was too big for her body. Carefully, like a child might wonder at the butterfly on her fingers. "This solitude has made me thirsty. Bring me something other than the water from the stream. If it pleases me, I'll tell you my story."

"What you got to do is water down his drink, Evita," Her aunt Cecilia told her, as she plopped herself down on a rickety stool. "He won't be none the wiser. Drunks like that, they don't do it for the taste."

Eva hummed as she moved rice around the pan on the stove. She did not want to hear them, the many remedies that could help her husband. If the unspoken truth before had made her stomach this, being this month's chisme was like a stab to her gut.

"Does he beat you?" Her aunt Lencha asked, tossing another log into the fire.

"No, tía!" Eva snapped her head to see the old woman crushing morro seeds with a cloth. "He's just...well, you know. *Nicolás.*"

"Eh, you could have it worse."

"Dios mio, Cecilia!" Aunt Lencha gasped and threw a dirty rag at her older sister's face. "Don't mind her, corazón. She's just a bitter old hag."

"Like you are any better?" She kissed her teeth. "Not every man can be your papi, got rest his soul. Mamá knew how to raise men who wouldn't drink or gamble. Kept them in line. Your mother won that lottery with Quique. Your tía and I married animals. But thank God, those sons of bitches died young. Women were put on this Earth to suffer."

"Do you really believe that?" It was hardly the first time Eva heard that sentiment. If it wasn't the aunts then it was every other woman in town, not even thinking about her words. Said in deep breaths over afternoon coffee, not even whispered.

"It's not about belief, mi niña," Aunt Cecilia said, with a defeated look to her. "It's the natural order of things. See if the bull has birthing pains. If he raises his calf. It's the same with men."

It was pointless to press her aunts further, she realized. They had never been young, Eva thought. They had always slaved over their stoves and ovens with puckered lips, running after the sons that quickly escaped their grasp.

"They didn't have any sweet oranges at the market," Eva thought to distract them with the horchata. "Are limes alright?"

The aunts waved the concern away and said no more. It was better that way, to leave out questions as to why Eva had asked them for a drink so cold this late in the year. Better than the water from the stream, those had been the terms. Guaro and wine were tainted with the bitterness of Eva's shame. No, Lilit would reject such a thing. She would taste humiliation and resentment in it. It needed to be something that quenched thirst and filled the belly.

When it was done Eva poured it into a metal thermos and carried it with the care afforded to newborns. She made the familiar trek with it on her back, her chest swollen with anticipation. With need. It deepened when she found Lilit, bathing herself in moonlight. Eva thought about setting the offering down and getting on her knees. Instead, Lilit took it and drank from it with an urgency that dried Eva's mouth, making her wish she could drink from her lips.

"You see?" Lilit laid on the grass and stretched out. Like a cat that had grown pleased with its mistress. "Pride makes everything better, like a pinch of salt."

No one had spoken to her like that. Without the pity, without reprimand. It was an odd sort of kindness, to be seen. To be caught in Lilit's gaze as she joined her on the ground.

"You owe me then," Eva told her, feeling a rare burst of confidence. "More than a sentence, you did not think to leave one drop for me."

"I'm no swindler, not like the Devil your people are so fond of." Lilit laid a hand on her side, squeezed until she found bone. Her touch made Eva shudder and then, lean into it.

"You were ripped from man's side," She whispered into her ear. "Or so the story goes. But I...I was made before he was. I was made from the earth between roots and streams. He was made from the brittle dirt of droughts."

Eva found the courage to feel the outline of her jaw. The bridge of her nose, the perfect angles that could have only been designed. Light barely penetrated the thickness of the clouds so she committed every detail of Lilit to her memory.

"Man, you see," She continued with a sigh. "Was born with a certain discontent. Perhaps it is the brokenness that first created the universe that lies within him. It was not enough that he ruled the land next me, that command of beasts and waters was ours. He had to possess it, to try and fill that emptiness. When lions and wolves grew boring, he turned his sights on me."

You have it so easy, Evita. I break the skin of my knuckles to put food on the table, all you have to do is keep house. Would you at least lie back and let me get off? She had believed him, had felt ungrateful all these years. Guilty for not wanting him, for being repulsed. For resenting his breath on her neck, the brutish grunts. Without realizing it, she let out a strangled sob of relief. He was unnatural, she realized. Against the way of the world. The order of the universe.

Lilit cocked her head to the side and waited for her to speak.

"How did you escape?" Eva asked her, hoping that there would be another ancient truth she could have.

"I made a knife and cut into his belly when he threw me to the ground," She chuckled, and removed Eva's hand from her face. "Before he could blame me, and be granted mercy from the Endless One, I fled."

The scene became an intricate painting in her mind's eye. Like the ones she had only seen photocopied in black and white in her public-school textbooks. Lilit's naked figure, and the blood oozing from Man. The crude knife in her grasp, the beasts surrounding their mistress. Lapping up the blood on the grass, baring their teeth at their tormentor. Eva could see Lilit being taken on a lion's back, guarded by a pack of wolves on her way out.

"My name has been a curse ever since," She turned her gaze in the direction of Concepción. "Invoked only when Man needs to be frightened"

It was no curse, she wanted to say. To be a thing to be feared, to be spoken about in hushed tones. Better than her name be on everyone's lips. *Evita, Evita, you're so good. So soft, would you watch my baby? Would you bake some quesadillas? Oh, but my mama said you wouldn't take money. Evita, Evita, would you palm some tortillas? Don't trouble your little mind, Evita.*

"Make me like you."

"Ah, what would you give me for that?" Lilit played with the hairs at the nape of Eva's neck. "That I have never done."

"My soul." Eva replied without question.

"Don't be ridiculous," She laughed with her whole body, it echoed across the mountain. "You cannot sell what doesn't belong to you."

"What, then?" She heard the urgency in her voice, but it was without shame. "Something that isn't ridiculous. Something that's mine to give."

"The night is cold. And I have been out here for far too long. Make me warm and you can have anything you want, Eva."

It was an incantation coming from her lips. Lips, she knew, had been shaped by Divinity itself. Eva kissed them, parted them with her own. Fire sparked in her belly; her body became tighter and tighter. Lilit welcomed her tongue, Eva's roaming fingers. The hands that undressed her and the mouth that took her breasts. Eva felt her skin grow warm, like clay in her hands. She was so perfect inside—she could spend eternity making Lilit's voice hoarse with pleasure.

"Why be Lilit when you can be Eva?" She asked, after Eva lied spent, next to her on the grass. "Stay with me, here on this mountain."

"What would you offer me for that?"

"The world between these pines."

FOUR POEMS
by Cynthia Gallaher

Neysa McMein, American
Illustrator 1888-1949

Little Marjorie held out hands to her mother,
to memory of an Irish grandmother,
disabled women who racked up
wheelchair hours in church.

A crooked smile to her father and Scottish grandfather,
disabling men who squandered
their printers' wages
in Quincy, Illinois, bars.

On Kentucky Street,
she played schoolgirl porch salon hostess,
divvied cookies and lemonade
among neighborhood children,

While her parents, ill and sullen Belle,
drunken Henry, barely scraped together
supper for her
after everyone had gone.

Little Marjorie stared down at her hands, up at clouds,
imagined a pleasing palette of girl-like-her pictures,
with perfectly painted lives, legs and legacies
that led like a chain of paper dolls east.

Quincy locals funded Marjorie's art classes in Chicago,
While she plied church-learned piano skills
in the city's silent film theaters, a bucket of tips
placed ample brushes, paints and rolls of paper in her hands.

Independent from necessity,
a pioneer, with nowhere left to go,
she ran open-armed to New York,
to embrace her lost youth,

In smudged smock,
disheveled hair, she paused for a moment,
whipped pastel magazine covers
chalked as if a sidewalk's rainbow far from Quincy.

Above New York streets, she crafted
illustrations, ads and portraits,
and through each, endeavored not to repeat
hometown traditions of drunkenness, hunger or injury.

From her studio salon, childlike at her easel,
she led evening play with Algonquinites,
rallied local wit, encouraged composers,
stoked national enthusiasm for games of Charades.

And as suffragette for
women's right to vote,
led suffragette parades as flag bearer
down New York's 5th Avenue.

She even created the first image of Betty Crocker,
until then, only a name on a box, an invisible domestic spirit,
that she materialized from her blend
of 35 test-kitchen worker, real women's faces.

While Midwest roots left their traces, she was
little Marjorie no more—now Neysa, a name inspired
by numerology, her independence out of necessity,
a pioneer, with a new destination.

An artist and icon who
recreated her own womanly image
from scratch, with an open-to-others heart
and hands that never learned to cook.

೧೦೦೪

American Geisha
Chicago Style

She couldn't land a modeling job
at this warehouse of Japanese artifice,
photo studio of metamorphic rooms,
chilly sets of furniture, appliances,
bed linens, seamless photo paper,
each elaborately draped with Nordic models six feet tall,
with unshorn blond hair, Arctic eyes,
noses straight as scalpels.
She, perhaps too ordinary,
too warm and monochromatic to a panoramic lens
to prevent someone from just turning the ad page.

Idle chit-chat in the waiting room,
wised account execs to her dean's list skills,
but also skills to mix Manhattans, Martinis, Mimosas,
play pool and deal cards.
With holidays nearing, one exec observed,
"You're a girl men can talk to."
"Report to this address on Thursday night,"
she was told. "But wear a short skirt, lots of lipstick."

Throughout December, she tended bar
at the studio's weekly condo parties,
annual holiday thank yous to favored clients;
Ad agency and department store art directors,
twelve men each Thursday, ushered in for drinks,
buffets of filet mignon, chicken teriyaki, flaming desserts.
"There are no other women?" she asked.
"They'll drop by later," the Japanese/American host chuckled.
"Until then, keep these boys entertained and oiled."

She mixed and served and smiled and made small talk and told them
of college, games of chance and carting a portfolio, seeking her
fortune, listened to stories of products, parody and paternity suits.
"Where'd you learn to mix such a wicked Margarita?
You're probably not old enough to drink yourself," one said.
He was right, she was only 19, and gave thanks to her stepdaddy,
a man who worked prohibition taverns on Blue Island Avenue
and taught her the bar trade while other kids toyed
with chemistry sets, Easy-Bake ovens.

Dinner was over, doors swept open,
three women in gowns and fur coats
which she could never afford,
whirled in from the outdoor freeze.

She was ushered off to a corner pool table with three clients,
the small bar where she stood, now transformed to narrow stage
for each of the wintery women,
who peeled wooly after filmy layer from their supple bodies.
 Perpendicular, the bartendress hit isosceles and parallograms
to opponents' dizzying chagrin,
players drank shots for every bumper she smacked.
While nine other chaps leapt for G-strings
from cinemascopic strippers,
her small, captive circle took careful cues
as if each deft stroke and movement were action shots
the photo studio couldn't replicate;
Though yet to make it in the modeling biz,
she was hailed as Straight Shooter of the Sloe Gin Fizz.

Gigolo Pantoum

I've ridden Chicago "L" trains since age 13,
and nothing like this ever happened before,
to be propositioned right as the train sped downtown
and reach Medicare status before those words transpired.

Nothing like this ever happened before,
I parked my car in a fancier neighborhood than I live,
I reached Medicare status, that's what my driver's license says,
I wanted to get on the train closer to downtown.

I parked my car in fancy Lincoln Park,
his friends told him it was the train stop where rich gals boarded,
I wanted to get on closer to downtown, not get off,
he wore an ironed khaki shirt, was young and good-looking.

His friends told him go to the north side for some bored, rich marks,
we know how to sell drugs, you know how to talk to women,
you're too good-looking, tall and pressed brother not to be a gigolo,
he saw me from across the train aisle and approached me.

He wasn't on drugs, and in a kind-of-shy, talk-to-women way,
he cradled the pole next to me & said, "Can I ask you a question?"
I didn't see him from across the aisle as he approached me,
he seemed lost as if about to ask directions, and I said, "Yes?"

There was something respectful about the way he said, "Can I ask you a question?"
was he a male model, perhaps heading downtown for a booking?
ah, I looked like I knew the city, and yes, I could help with directions,
then he drew his face closer and said, "Are you interested in a relationship?"

I remembered decades of eager males I knew, downtown and otherwise,
and for a split second I thought he was serious, and I said "Sorry."
but those words "interested" and "relationship" carried financial subtext,
and I woke up and said, "No," then really woke up to brush him off.

He sent me back decades and for a second I thought he was serious,
I was wearing a nice dress & good sandals, but he knew I was older,
I woke up as if finally getting the punch line and waved my hand, like stop already,
but I imagined he saw me through my own young eyes and best get-up.

He knew I was older, forget the dress, the shoes, the freshly washed hair,
I told my husband, I'm having a hard time making this gigolo story a poem,
I imagined he had seen me the way my husband still sees me all these years,
come here, said my husband, I'll give you a gigolo story.

I texted my husband from the train, a gigolo story is unfolding on the brown line,
my cousin said, he could at least have taken the Metra for a little class,
I told her my gigolo story has class cause it involves me, thank you,
it's not about you, my husband said, the guy needs money to survive.

He could have taken the Metra but they charge you each way,
instead, he keeps going around the Loop, getting on again at the end of the line,
it's not about you, it's me, it's not about me, it's you, it's not about relationships,
it never happened to me before because I wasn't old enough.

He keeps going round the Loop, getting on again at the end of the line,
to proposition one who may say "Yes" as the train speeds downtown,
it never happened to me before because I wasn't old enough,
even though I've ridden Chicago "L" trains since age 13.

ജഉഈ

Woman at the Water Park
Merrillville, Indiana

I learn the names, ages of her children,
and her pipefitter husband's special handle, "Tank."

I learn details of her back porch saloon
and its demolition,
she and Tank both quit drinking together
two years ago.

The turning point in their relationship:
Winning a trip for two to the Turks and Caicos
through 103.5 FM, The Beat.

It served as a perfect honeymoon—
the couple were married poolside after 10 years of common law,
the hotel with a swim-up bar,
a wet celebration with Virgin Margaritas and Virgin Pina Coladas,
and later, a round bed, plenty of birth control,
each already with their own kids and each other's.

She lay languid at the water park now, bronzed on the lounge chair,
I reflect on her, she's pretty; with firm legs, long sandy hair,
except for a small pot belly from three kids, years of beer,
except when she leaps up again to open a sun-dried mouth,
spouting double negatives and light, but good-natured curses;
an unlit cigarette dangles there.

She's from Hegewisch,
they now live in Hobart, a step up.
"But Tank here wants to move even farther away,"
she said, placing her hand lovingly on his knee.
"What the hell, he wants to keep me safe."

Yet during this far-flung reprieve in Deep River Water Park,
they're still up to their necks in minor terrors.
I tell her some teens stole their inner tubes
while they were off to the pizza cabana.

I know much about her already,
yet she's forgotten we weren't introduced,
but sometimes a woman's story is
more vital than her name.

Her son Eddie, 14, a towel wrapped around his hips,
waves on route to another water slide, with her daughter Tammy, 12.
"From my previous marriage of eight years to an abuser,"
she whispers confidentially. "I never said anything," she said.
"I thought, 'He'll change.' Then I met Tank."

Tank peers over his sunglasses,
grunts as he sets aside a tall ice tea,
extends a meaty hand,
then beams a wide boyish grin.

✎☙☜✎

THREE POEMS
by Tanya Ko Hong

The War Still Within

Tonight my tongue cuts galaxy
black bones be fire
a crying cello drifting
if I open my mouth
I will be sent to the Taklimakan
Desert a graveyard
silence of a thousand skulls
Endless black
Nothing can live
My eyes a flame
I never talk about the battleground
My secret burns there
My silence is your mouth
My skull the house of story
My jaw hinges
star-dirt
devastation in a capsule

White man said
> *No one listens to you*
> *No one sees*
> *Open your mouth*

I said

Go ahead
Cut and burn my tongue
You can't set fire to my secrets
My other tongue
will speak

I carry my eyes, my bones
through this war

"The Reincarnation of Mother Teresa as an Elephant"
by David Sheskinhazmat

Do you still believe in spring?

A lonely bird knocks on a kitchen window
Open the window

Is there still a world? Deserted school
playground, buttercup lip gloss, unopened,

cold french fries, uncertain future
Hope like rotten lemon juice

An ambulance siren sings
Red and white glitter against

sidewalks Tonight someone dies
alone A patch of lotus

flowers exude fragrance
Sunrise yellow, tea green, salmon pink

Though some think it dead, its seeds
can germinate for thousands of years

Later the lotus blooms
magnificent in the deepest mud

I pray this poem finds in your darkness,
hands reaching through ghost light

In the remaining space of this postcard
I write, I still believe in love

*Inspired by the students of my Fairfax High Poetry Workshop during
pandemic*

Waiting

When I think of you, rain comes
When I call you, you come in rain
When I touch you, you disappear
in rain

Bring me raw garlic and a handful
of bitter green wormwood
I will eat them and stay in a cave
21 days, 100 days
that's how bear became woman
I will do the same
        If I can see you one last time.

There is another myth—
When you fold one thousand paper cranes
your dream comes true
If I can see you one last time
I will fold thousands—
        ten thousand paper cranes

I want to open your apartment door again
with the key that you sent by mail,
the key still warm from your hand,
hang my clothes in your closet between your clothes—
        I want to feel safe there again

Waiting for you is nothing—
Without blinking, I watch
the night become silver rain in blue light

I will wait for you like a rock on the water line
wishing you to be a wave and reach me—
If you touch
I will collapse and be water like you.

"Perfection" by Karen Boissonneault-Gauthier

TEMPORARY GHOSTS
by Heather Fowler

Leigh arrived in the after-death waiting room moments after her heart stopped beating. One moment, normalcy, and the following, catecholaminergic polymorphic ventricular tachycardia. She'd heard the paramedics call out her declining vitals.

Before this, she'd been undiagnosed, so there was transport in an unexpected exit, but it was awful to be robbed of reality so suddenly.

The Temporary Ghosts Waiting Room, where she next found herself, was both boring and baffling. She had no idea why she was there, or even where "there" was. Still, she could not be expected to know anything about the Afterlife before reaching the Afterlife. Nonetheless, the ugly room, occupied by a handful of other newly dead, saddened her with its pale gray walls the color of ruined erasers. Spanning its lengths were long wooden benches where the occasional newly-dead pamphlet had been scattered. "You, too, can go Perm Official!" these pamphlets said, though this was not the top choice since they also said. "Perm Official Status means Lifetime Servic e in the Investigatory Sector. In another life, you may Re-Pool."

But the sign on the locked inner door said *Temporary Ghosts* and through its embedded window, Leigh viewed the intervening room. The people in that room cued into fastidious lines. Many held e-clipboards, filling out forms with short black styluses.

Unruly children were assisted by clerks with diffuser shots, yet even there the mood seemed cheerfuler, and Leigh felt a strong pull to leave.

"I don't want to be a Temporary Ghost!" she shouted. "I want to go into the other room!"

No one replied. So she yanked at the locked door, prepared to beat against it, but just then, a man with a clipboard opened it, so her fists fell on his soft open chest with three dull thuds.

"You're free to leave, Leigh," he said, stepping back to regard her like a rabid cat. "We'll know what to do with you soon enough."

As he spoke, a button must have been depressed from a remote location because, like magic, the far wall, which had appeared as brick, split apart to reveal a niched opening where yellow light flooded in.

"Don't go too far from the waiting room," the man continued. "Remember, you're still in-process!"

At this, a chubby boy of eight in faded denims called out, "Me, too, still, Rucks? I've waited longest. Eight days this time! What's the hold up?"

"Limbo days again, Winston," the man replied. "And, as you well know, four Perms are currently out surveying your deeds."

"Bah bah bah!" the boy shouted, his front teeth chipped and prominent. "I hate Perms, you shifty bastards! I hate Temporary Ghosts. Rucks, I hate you!"

"You might, but you don't what comes next, so calm down," the man answered, his voice soft and ineffectual. "Go down the chute, Winston, as is your habit, but if you don't return when called, we'll put you in THE BLANCHER. Maybe you could stand to be Blanched."

Winston stood, assuming a terrified demeanor. "Yes, sir. I'll be back on time. Not THE BLANCHER, if you please."

"What's that?" Leigh asked. "What's THE BLANCHER? And where am I? And why is this child trapped here?"

"You're in the In Between," Rucks said. "The Transport Annex, which is the place between your most recent life and your next. Winston's a Temporary Ghost, just like you."

A married couple beside her snuggled and whispered in hushed tones until, "But now what?" the wife asked aloud. "What are our choices from here?"

"You'll be told when you're next called up," the administrator replied. "There's nothing we can tell you now that matters."

"Oh, yes, there is! I need our options more clearly, right now," the husband insisted. "I want to know!"

"Naturally, you want to know," the administrator said as he turned away, "but knowing now isn't one of your options. You may know some options in general, for example, like those from the pamphlet, but not your specific ones—because they haven't yet been determined. This is why you are a Temporary Ghost. Thank you very much and goodbye." Then the man Rucks smiled once more and left the room.

As he did, the door relocked behind him with a *whoosh* and a *click*. Several others began to shout for sooner results, too, but, "They won't give you any more than you already got," the boy Winston said coolly, standing on one of the benches and walking a straight line on top, heel to toe, heel to toe. "I've been here several times. Listen, least Rucks opened the door and came in this time. He doesn't always. So we might as well go home before they come back. Or see some stuff. Good times! My teeth don't even hurt here."

"See some stuff where?" Leigh asked.

"You could see the Re-Pool, for THE BIG SWIM," Winston said. "Tour the Transport Annex. Fine. You do that. But I'm going home, while I still can, out the chute. Home."

"Home," Leigh echoed. It was neither question nor a statement, more a faded cousin of a sob. She pulled her fingers through her dirty auburn hair and repeated, like it was a foreign land, "Home..."

"Yeah. Home. Where you once stayed comfortably, or not so comfortably, among the living," Winston replied. "Last chance for bad folks to see 'home' is now. If they figure you're bad, they'll vaporize you, which is to say, they'll use THE BLANCHER. That pain is supposed to be worse than giving birth or having dental work."

"But how do they know if I'm bad?" Leigh stammered, fascinated by his attitude and his firm pronouncements.

"Oh," he said. "They always know. Or they figure it out." And he spoke with such an arrogance it made him the kind of know-it-all kid she hated teaching in her classes, a kid who has no respect. *Am I bad that I didn't like all my students,* she then thought, *that I wanted to cudgel some?*

"But, maybe they won't know anything about me," she replied.

"Ha. Ha. Didn't you hear Rucks?" Winston rejoined. "They investigate." He walked toward the exit and Leigh followed until, "Bug off, lady," Winston said. "Because you're not going where I'm going, so you can't follow."

"I might be," she replied. "How would you know?"

"Fine. Follow me into my life if you want," he said. "But I'm sure it's not my old house you want to see, and the chute will take you elsewhere anyway. It listens. As for me, I'm gonna play with old toys. Gonna find a green down chute, and get the heck out of here. Any minute."

He strode out and began to survey the exterior. Leigh reached for his shoulder, wanting to beg for help, but he yanked himself away with an angry tug, so she tried to scare him, saying, "My name is Leigh. You're going to THE BLANCHER if you don't help me. Not helping people makes you a bad person!"

"I will not!" he shouted. "It does not! They only look at what we did before, so stop talking!" But Winston then bit his lip and started crying, so she realized how young he was.

"Oh, I'm sorry, sweetheart," she said. "I really didn't mean it. But if you leave now, how will you know when to come back?" Her voice was softer this time, more encouraging.

He wiped his face. "We just know when to come back," he said. "If you're here, you'll feel the pull toward the waiting room. If you're not, well... ZZZZZZZZZZZRRRRRRRRRRSPPP! This." He reached into his pocket and pulled out a small electric device, adding, "It buzzes hard when they want you. Dig around. You have one."

Leigh reached into her pocket and found a buzzer. "Thanks, kid," she said.

"No problem," he replied, again grinning his cocky grin, but he touched her arm and winked once before whispering conspiratorially, "I can see you're wondering how to move around. So, if you really want to go home, just jump into the nearest chute and think real hard about

See, there's one opening over there! But lady, listen, no one can see you or hear you when you're a Temporary Ghost, so don't go trying to talk to anyone."

She nodded.

"Only the dead hear the dead," he went on. "Or a few clairvoyants. But lots of faker psychics can't hear shit. Boris said that."

"Who?"

"One of my *other* souls," Winston said. "Don't you have any?"

"I don't know."

"Then you don't.   If you did, you would have heard them by now," Winston said. Then he walked toward a shimmering green cylinder fifty yards away.

"I probably haven't heard from any yet because I'm not sure I'm dead," she said. "I'm probably not. Maybe I'm only half dead? I could come back to life any second, like when the paramedics shock you back?"

"No, only fully dead people come here," he replied.

"You're wrong," she rebutted and stared down at her cream blouse, her chocolate slacks and heels. "I'm probably only dreaming this death— because I don't look dead." She even believed herself, feeling perfectly put together, regardless that the last moment she actually recalled had been spent in an ambulance, listening to her own flat line.

Winston scoffed. "Okay, lady. Check your pulse," he said. "You don't have one, so obviously I'm calling it. Heads. You're dead." He then flipped an imaginary coin and dropped a palm over where it would have landed, feigning surprise and lifting his hand, saying, "See! Heads up, you're dead! But also, tails up, you're dead. And trust me: You won't look like anything to the Livers. You'll be the palest clear air they'll walk through. They might feel a little chill, but all you can do as a Temporary Ghost is watch and wait."

"For what?"

"Depends," he said, pumping his fingers in a fist as a wave goodbye. "People wait for just about anything, I guess. But I gotta go. Say, Leigh, last tip, because I've been here before: Don't let the investigators get in your head." He then walked into his chute and shouted, "Toodles!" before shooting down through the light before the chute disappeared.

Frantically, Leigh looked for another chute or even for another person, but the others must have remained in the waiting room, so she stood on the place of Winston's former chute, wishing for it to reappear, but it didn't. Then, she walked half a mile to the next structure, which was an enormous facility labeled THE BIG SWIM. It was the only thing anywhere nearby.

From outside, the door was locked, but she saw through huge picture windows where hundreds of people in unusual swimsuits entered a pool at the shallow end closest to the door, noticing they strode down the pool stairs into the water, clutching the rail, then swam, strong as they might, toward the pool's farthest end. At some point, though, before the other side, each disappeared like schools of teeming fish at the edge of a waterfall cliff, visible then gone.

How they swam at all with so little room between, baffled Leigh. She had the sense of watching an entire population vanish into a void. "Where have they gone?" she asked a stylish woman who suddenly appeared beside her in a svelte black dress.

"To their other lives, of course," the woman said. "Their next ones."

Leigh regarded the woman with greater interest. "You locked out, too?"

"No," the woman said sharply. "Just deciding what to do. I could go in, or I could take an Official Role, investigating. The BIG SWIM's a crapshoot. You get in, and there's no telling who'll you'll end up with. You could be an incapacitated child—or a stillbirth. It's not THE BLANCHER, which takes your past souls, but it's still a risk." Her dismay was palpable.

"And if you investigate?" Leigh asked.

"You stay here, as you were," the woman said. "Haunting the living, so to speak, deciding the fates of iffy people like yourself: Are they good eggs or bad? But at least you have a space to come home to when you're done. I couldn't figure out what to say on my e-clipboard: Did I want to stay—or join a new life? I didn't know. No rush in deciding, they said.

Take your time and walk around... But why aren't you in the buildings? Are you deciding, too?"

"Oh. No," Leigh said. "They say I'm a Temporary Ghost now, I guess. So I don't decide. They do."

"Oh," the woman said. "Wonder what they question about you... How'd you die?"

"Heart attack."

"And were you stealing when you kicked the bucket? Killing? Ransacking something?"

"No," Leigh replied.

"Okay, then, you destroyed someone?"

"No." Leigh stared off into the buttery yellow sky with no sun or stars, just a halogen haze. "At least I don't think so."

"Usually, you know," the woman said. "Or are at least aware of one terrible thing you've done."

"I don't think I'm deliberately terrible," Leigh said. "I don't ever hurt anyone on purpose."

"Okay, so maybe you're fine," the woman said. "Perfect on all counts. But, I doubt it. Oh, well. They'll investigate... I thought for sure I'd go to THE BLANCHER straight off since I'm a bad ass bitch, but I didn't. They say it's instant for the truly terrible."

Leigh watched more swimmers enter the blue water and disappear, a rainbow of flesh and garments dropping into azure. At the pool's far end, what appeared to be white chemicals were dumped just beyond where swimmers disappeared. "So many bodies in there," she mused. "Wonder if that's chlorine poured in the far end to keep it safe and hygenic. They keep doing that."

"Chlorine for ghost bodies?" black dress lady asked and laughed. "Not a chance. It's Blanched souls. Post-Blancher. They'll have a time of it in their next lives, innocent as babes. But new souls are so boring."

Leigh regarded a slight pilling on her skirt, pulled on it. "How do you know?"

"Just look at them," the woman replied. "All white and blobby. You can see they've got no collective memory."

"Is that why they're so pale?"

Black dress woman laughed again. "Of course it is. Not a trace of who they were remains. By the way, you can self-elect THE BLANCHER if you want... But who wants that? Who wants to go back to being new? Whole lot of nothingness in that!" She stared at the swimmers and sighed. "That's why you take THE BIG SWIM, or didn't you hear? To keep your old soul or souls... Have you even met yours? Are they nice?"

"I haven't," Leigh said, wondering if this was a common topic around here. "But I'd like to, and if I had, I'd take THE BIG SWIM to save them and take them with me. If I knew who they were, if I liked them."

"Ah, well, if they haven't started talking to you here, then you probably don't have any," the woman said. "I have twelve. But, darling, you don't know what you'll take with you anywhere. Because you're a Temporary Ghost with only one soul, clearly, so the one soul you have must have done something pretty bad. That's interesting. Very. Maybe you were Blanched in the life before this? Maybe you always need Blanching."

Leigh looked away. "You should be an Investigator, lady," she said. "You have a knack." But a new chute appeared just fifty yards away, so Leigh strode toward it as the woman continued to examine her.

The chute radiated green and purple. "Think of home," Leigh reminded herself and fell into a wavering light just before whizzing through the sky and down to an earthly sinkhole before appearing on the steps of her former brownstone.

She walked to the building's entry door and grasped at the knob, but her hand fell through it. Without thinking, she then walked through the door, but, she couldn't fly, she next discovered, so she waited for an elevator with riders who would press the buttons before finally getting off with Mrs. Nebitz at her and Hideo's old floor.

Hideo. Her lover. Where was he now? And would he see her?

A newspaper on her doormat announced it was a week after her death, August the 10th. Happy August the 10th, she thought, an old Tennessee Williams story occurring to her then. She'd died on August the 3rd.

But when she walked through a second door to enter her place, she found Hideo, splayed nude on the floor. Afternoon light streamed through bay windows, and below him were her clothes. A shake of his torso alerted her he did not sleep. His buried face revealed he sobbed, burrowing into her things, with his neck curled toward his chest.

As she watched him this way, having nothing better to do, she noted he stayed this way for hours. Then he went about his manlier business, putting on undergarments and tan slacks, making green tea, watching his favorite television shows, and answering his phone.

"I'm on bereavement leave," she heard him tell someone. But his phone kept dialing out. From his side of the conversations, it sounded like he planned a funeral. Hers. "Four bouquets of red chrysanthemums," he ordered, because he knew she loved those cheap cousins of roses. He spoke of caskets. Once, he picked up a picture of her and pressed his index finger to the glass. "Leigh," he said.

"It's me!" she said, "I'm here, Hideo! I'm sorry I left..." but he couldn't hear her. He couldn't see her. Not even when she stood right before his face and tried to kiss him but had no mass. Then she saw another ghost appear beside her, a thirteen year old in a bright purple dress with tiny freckles and red braids.

"He loved you so much," the girl said. "I've watched him for days and days. Every day, it's the same. Cry a little. Masturbate. Get dressed. Have his tea. He hasn't left this place at all."

"Why do you investigate him?" Leigh said. "He's not me. He's done nothing wrong!"

"Oh, watching him here is not about him," the girl replied while both watched Hideo linger at the fridge, standing before the nearly empty shelves and staring in. "It's about you."

It hurt Leigh to see him suffer this way, but it also made her angry how the investigator violated his privacy.

"What privacy?" the girl asked, hearing Leigh's thoughts. "He can't see me or hear me. And watching him is a shell game since now we're watching you watching him. It's you we're looking at, Leigh, through reactions to him and how you behave. Are you a person worth missing this much?"

"Sometimes I am," Leigh said.

"Right. Also of interest," the girl continued. "Like when you're not. Thinking here about those plane tickets you bought to Canada. How you closed your emails to that guy Greg. Then that other strange man's mouth on your neck on the subway, the man you didn't even know-- while you were engaged to Hideo. How you stood and enjoyed it when the stranger's hand slipped into your pants. Then, too, we consider your trip to 23rd street last year when you were pregnant and bled out your baby but didn't go to a doctor. When you carried Hideo's child but had planned to get rid of it even before it left. The way you refused to wear Hideo's engagement ring on the 7 train. So, were you a good person, or a bad person in life, Leigh? Tell us that. That's what we need to know. And do you need to be Blanched?"

"Miscarriage isn't murder," Leigh said. "And I'm not a bad person for failing to fall in love. For having doubts. Hideo and I weren't married."

"But isn't a miscarriage murder when you arguably tried to make it happen with drugging and drink? And how bad should we consider those emotional infidelities? You would have married him regardless?"

"Don't talk about those things with him around," Leigh replied. "They're ugly. And he's not."

"But are you?" the girl asked. "Really?"

"No," Leigh replied. "I stopped at the critical line. I never went to Canada. Never let those kisses or copped feels turn into rooms." She thought of Greg, how she'd almost taken a trip to him to leave Hideo forever. But almost was almost. Almost wasn't a completed deed.

"Which is why you're a Temporary Ghost, and a maybe," the girl investigator said. "So maybe you'll get a choice in this afterlife, and maybe not. But weren't you glad to die, Leigh? Let's talk about that some. Why were you so joyful to leave your body? Most people aren't. That's curious."

I had nothing to live for, Leigh thought. *I would never have killed me, but to escape was like heaven.*

"So, you just wanted it over with, is that all?" girl investigator said. "All the daily struggles. All your mediocre accomplishments and multi-plying fear..."

"It was more," Leigh said.

"Explain it to me…"

Leigh tried but had no suitable response. What were the words one could use for the feeling of not wanting to die but not wanting to live. Being tired of failure and disappointment. Being tired of being expected to be more. For living abject misery without speech? She wanted to pull the girl's braid very hard and run, to scream, to do anything to get the prying presence out of her mind. She didn't want to answer. She wasn't going to answer.

"If you want me out so much, then shut your mental door!" girl investigator murmured. "But, ah, I get it. I suppose you've never been investigated before, so your mental door's wide open. A stampede could trample through. Shall I tell you what I see in your thoughts, Leigh? What I found below the even the layer that you listen to yourself? I see you found Hideo hideous and couldn't really love him. I see you were afraid he was the only one who'd love you forever, so you kept him, but were never satisfied--and this is why you took off your engagement ring in public, in case there could be more—also why you were strangely glad to die. It kept you from betrayal or suicide, didn't it? Saved from flawed love, self-hate, and fate by your own bad heart! How ironic! And you never saw yourself finding anyone you could truly love. But why, Leigh? Why?"

Because I chose badly once and I can't do it again, Leigh thought. *Ever.* Guilt caromed though her. "Yes, I hid in my life with Hideo," she said. "Because life doesn't always happen the way you want it to. People you love don't love you back. Maybe you're a good person only drawn to the worst kind of people. So, stability is worth something, isn't it? Caring can be worth everything. Don't you agree?"

"No, lady. What a cop out! You have to make your life how you want it," investigator girl said. "You gave up trying to find true love after the crazy one cut out your faith and joy in mankind. You chose to keep teaching children, which you didn't enjoy. Everything was half measures. It's okay. Admit it. And don't think I can't see that time you locked yourself in the teacher's bathroom and did the Special K because you were bored and unhappy. Took the edge off that day, didn't it? Want more? You can have it in the Afterlife. But there's a catch…"

In the girl's open palm, a mound of pale powder appeared, which she flung in the air, but it disappeared. "It's an illusion. Besides," the girl said, "You get no high from drugs after death. You have no blood pumping. Because you're dead, Leigh. Dead."

"Get out of my head!" Leigh shouted, insistent now, terrified now, desperate since Hideo had began to rub his body on her garments again and masturbate on them right as they watched.

"You want me out, then shut the mental door!" the girl shouted back. "I already told you how!"

But Hideo, sobbing, distracted them both. "I'm so sorry, Hideo," Leigh said. "I'm so sorry I never loved you enough." And as she said this, a chute appeared between Leigh and the investigator, so *Home*, she thought walking into it. *Home, somewhere else please*—though was unsure where she meant. And then she fell in the chute and went to the only other home she'd been thinking about in days. Winston's.

Within seconds, she stood in a suburban boy's bedroom as Winston lounged on the carpet and built Legos, humming a nervous tune. "Hey, what are you doing here, Leigh?" he asked, looking up. "This isn't your place."

"They're investigating me, Winston," she whispered. "I had to escape. They went to my lover's, and..."

"Read your mind?" he predicted.

"Yes! Very unpleasant!"

"Right. Okay, but don't take things so hard," he said, smiling with his chip-toothed smile. "We're still Temp Ghosts, or we would have already been Blanched. You know where the investigators are now?"

"No."

"Probably in your old elementary school, looking. Maybe checking out your best friends' houses. Did you ever screw one over? They hate that. If they find nothing there, maybe they'll bop over to your parents' and scan their memories. If you did something awful to them, or anyone, anywhere, they'll go back to the moment and scene of that event, scan the spectators, and make a decision."

"And what if there weren't any spectators for the worst of what I did?" Leigh asked.

"Then they'd just watch you. Lucky you. Check out your lonely past."

"But I'm not in my past. I'm here, where they can't find me!"

"No," he corrected. "Now you're in two places. Actually, honey, you're in a trillion. Hold on, that was Boris talking. Wait! Now Emily says, 'Every place you've ever been is fair game—where you left your energy's echo'"

But something buzzed in Winston's pocket. His beeper. "Bye for now," he said. "I've got to go. Wish me luck."

"Luck," she replied, and when he vanished into a chute, she sat and played Legos for hours, making nothing she could identify, regretting the intense mess that was her life. But when a person has catecholaminergic polymorphic ventricular tachycardia, she thought, even if they didn't know it, they could go any time. What if she'd known she'd had this disease before her death—or, at some level, had always known? Would that have made a difference?

Feeling sorry for herself, she then determined: No. She'd only been in true love once and that had burned her so badly, it was impossible to repeat. But it had also been the only love that drew her in so fully. And it had been with a bad man, she acknowledged, a selfish, self-absorbed man, a sociopathological malignant whom no one should have loved, and yet he'd fooled many, she decided as she fitted a blue Lego into a red Lego and then a red Lego into a green, thinking: She hadn't done much of anything other than settling for something safe because her own desire terrified her, felt like a loaded gun aiming at a tank of gas known as life.

But many good people simply wouldn't find passionate love twice, she thought. And maybe the passion itself was self-destructive, the overload of emotions that led to the impossibility of self-care, all manifest from addictive personalities. After she stopped caring as much for Hideo, even his passion for her had grown self-destructive by clearly eclipsing her love for him, and that's why he'd suffered—since he felt so much more—while she might continue to feel almost nothing.

But he was a beautiful man, after all, she recalled, considering his tight, tan body. Though before him there were a string of other Hideos, and she'd caused them all so much pain, though this had left her cold every time. Was it because they were so good that they were boring? With each, she'd tried to find forevers, only finally calling halt to her own high body count path of decimation by saying, "Yes, I'll marry you, Hideo. I will."

And she'd tried so hard to make him feel she was in love, but that may be part of why she'd wanted to die. But the truth was she didn't trust who she'd choose next if let loose in the world again. She should not trust herself. "Shut this mental door," she told herself firmly, echoing the ghost girl. "Be quiet, Leigh. Be calm."

Then investigator girl appeared again with her hands on her hips, and said, "I wasn't even visible this time! How'd you know?"

"Oh, I didn't," Leigh replied. "I was talking to myself."

"All right. Well, I came to say it's time," the girl replied. "They're ready for you now."

Then Leigh's buzzer buzzed and a chute opened beside her. Once more, she dropped in. When she arrived back at the facility, this time, she landed in a cozier waiting room with lavender walls.

Rucks rolled in with a fat smile, in a green suit and tie. "Congratulations, Leigh!" he said. "You've been cleared. Keep your soul and Big Swim or Blanche it. Welcome to the Afterlife of Choice."

"What happened to Winston?" Leigh asked.

"Confidential, sorry. We can't disclose," Rucks replied.

"Did he get Blanched?"

"Now, now, don't ask about him. He was a bad kid," Rucks said. "He harmed others with little to no remorse. We can't talk details, but we can disclose that your care for Winston was helpful with deciding on yours. It was close! We even assessed that girl you cheated at cards and beat down in fifth grade. That time you almost drove off a cliff from sheer vanity. I mean bridge swerve is something we all consider at least once, right? You're not alone." Rucks laughed a geeky, complicit laugh before he whispered, "It's a good thing you turned yourself around, though, isn't it? Before your bad heart killed you."

"Guess so," Leigh responded, feeling the opposite. "But what did the woman in the black dress choose? Did she take The Big Swim?"

Rucks laughed again. "She stayed with you, of course. Chose to be thirteen again and investigate others through the veils of false youth. Red hair, long braids, violet frock; you know her. You can do that, too. If you want to be an investigator, you can be whatever age you want. Granted, it creeps people out, but it also disarms them. Anyway, if you want THE BIG SWIM, go get your swimsuit in your locker." He pointed to a locker bay. "Number 234559," he said. "Same combo."

Leigh walked toward it and Rucks followed. She opened the locker. Her suit inside was in her size, modest black spandex designed with rotting anatomical hearts. Each threaded heart had black spots.

She put on the suit and walked barefoot across the concrete room. As she did, she held an e-form on a clippie tablet Rucks had handed her. "Wait in the line, then leave it at the THE BIG SWIM counter if you want to go in," he said and she nodded, but five minutes later, she stood in THE BIG SWIM lobby, undecided, when she watched two men drag a kicking and hollering Winston into THE BLANCHER.

In the hallway, he glimpsed her briefly and shouted, "Hey, hey, Leigh! Fancy meeting you back here. ? Guess what? They want a whole new soul for me this time! Going to be Blanched! Hey, nice swimsuit!"

Then he laughed as they pulled the door shut behind him, his laughter pealing aloud until erased by its closure. Still, there was something charming and unrepentant in his tone. She had no idea what he'd done, but wondered: Why was she okay if he wasn't? Hadn't she, too, ruined lives? She could not know.

Through a viewing pane that connected the lobby to the infrastructure, she watched swimmers enter the pool, and just then, the woman in black/child investigator appeared beside her again, alternating between her teen girl self and older jaded self before finally choosing the older self with its black dress and spiky heels.

"You don't really want to swim," the woman told Leigh. "I've been in your head, and I'm not sure keeping this soul is right for you."

"I could investigate like you," Leigh replied. "Maybe stay here."

"That's not you either," the woman said. "Just not judgmental enough..."

"Maybe so," Leigh agreed, and both women watched as the men who tended the pool brought container after container of pale souls from THE BLANCHER to dump in the deep end. "I'll admit I never fully saw the value of THE BLANCHER before now!" the woman enthused. "Or in which circumstances it would be best... But, now I think about it and realize: if you get Blanched, you arrive like a fresh new being with no former sorrows. Sure, maybe you're a little bit boring because you're a new soul and people who haven't suffered have no depth, but you're oh so fresh and new. Your newe soul gets a do-over. That could be good."

"Thank you for your help," Leigh said. "But I'd like to be alone." And, *Shut the mental door,* she willed. In that moment, she heard it click and latch, visualizing her door as a metal patio gate with a deadbolt.

"Excellent work! Progress!" the woman said. "I can't see a thing you're thinking now. But, I've gotta go. My next assignment calls. A man who disowned all his kids since he couldn't feed them. Good luck, Leigh. Choose well." As she spoke, the woman flickered and returned to her little girl self. She smiled and waved then strode to an outdoor chute.

Leigh looked down at the anatomical hearts swimsuit. She stared at the throngs of newly dead swimming hard and dropping into new lives on the other end of the pool.

She looked, too, at the white souls dumped into the other end. Then she thought of a book she'd read once, *The Crime of Sylvestre Bonnard* by Anatole France, and she walked out of the pool admin area and entered THE BLANCHER.

Once inside, she dropped her suit on the floor and said, "I didn't need to be investigated. My choice was this, all along! I always wanted to be new."

But the moment she was Blanched was the most painful, startling, and liberating experience she'd ever had. Genderless, voiceless, there was only a thrum of concentrated energy now, so for a long time Leigh, or whatever she'd become, felt bathed in energy.

At the same time, in the distance, Hideo pressed his nose in her silky clothes. He moaned, stroking himself, still floating through the repulsive drain of his own thoughts, but cognizant and alive.

He had a good heart, not a thing wrong with it, she thought, but it was still as if he knew something was happening to her as she became a new nothingness in that moment, for just then he imagined himself on a great sea of nothingness, too, or as the great sea. Then he pulled on that part of himself in his hand that might have made a life, yanking on it ineffectually as he thought of her leaving and the stunning hole of loss he now fucked himself into.

But this was when Leigh, or the thing she'd become, was free, not even capable of remembering her last thoughts before the Blanching, which were all about how a woman needed to be strong enough to help her future, no matter the cost, to change her patterns and be reborn whenever a bad love caused too much pain—which echoed the quote by France in the book she remembered: "All changes, even the most longed for, have their melancholy...we must die to one life before we can enter another."

And that's what made it so clear in the end, what caused her to be Blanched and dumped into the deep-end as a pale white blob.

Now, whatever new soul came next would be fully clear of her check-ered past, floating innocent and light in the viscous mid, and, carrying no trauma, go back down there as a blameless babe, expel the fetal liquid from her lungs, have a good strong scream, and start again.

ꙮ

TWO POEMS
by Marisca Pichette

WRITE THIS DOWN
from Tyehimba Jess' Olio

Now, listen for once, and write this down: tame your fear like a
woman tames hers.

Her manicured hands clutch fear's teeth, her painted face soaks in
fear's breath, her pressed and molded hair bends under fear's saliva.
She takes fear in the face, and pushes him back.

We're told to fear the pain of birth—we keep on ripping the world
out of us.

We're told to fear a man—we keep on speaking up.

We're told to fear ourselves—we take hands and twist our fingers
together until they're breaking, screaming across the line of pain
and anguish and identity.

We weren't all born women; we don't all want to *be* women. Our
faces only make up half the wage we make, the other side melting
into tears that turn us into pillars of salt.

We march forward even as our legs crumble and harden, paling into crystals. We strain on, squeezing ourselves into the grip of the world, starving the salt from our veins.

We'll go on starving out the rest of our days, if that's what it takes. And we'll take the fear they gave us, and heal our pillared selves whole.

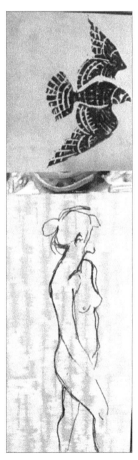

"Woman and Raven" by Cynthia Yatchman

bitches

bitches are like
    birdsong and Sun-In
    threadbare t-shirts, summer camp logos cracked
    gin and tonic on grandma's patio
   blackberry picking and scratches on hands warm from the sun,
    cold from the dew
    faded Converse and Vans spattered with manure.

bitches are like
    bralettes and underwire
    eyeliner and chapstick
    deodorant and orange peels
    coconut oil and dandruff
    cellulite and stretch marks
    Swiss chard and toothpaste.

bitches are like
    I love you
    I need you
    I need no one
    you complete me
    I am complete.

bitches are like
    rain and lightning
    screams and laughter
    sweaty feet and aching thighs
    broken fingers and split lips
    bondage and breakfast
    tortillas and fettucine
    tattoos and lip rings.

bitches like
>you
>me
>her
>them
>him
>us.

bitches like
>luck and what we found instead
>marches and staying home, using our ex's Netflix
>alone
>together
>marzipan and marsupials
>tea and chocolate
>vodka and Peeps
>tomorrow and two thousand years before we sang
>and felt heard
>two thousand years before that and
>two thousand years from now.

bitches are
>the future
>if futures still happen on a world
>where all of us
>can still be called

>*bitches.*

৩৩৩

SNAKE OIL
by Leigh Camacho Rourks

Manny'd changed the background on their computer again, and now deep blue waves curled around an island in the center of Lolo's screen. It looked like a jade carving set in spilled paint, the colors so saturated. She could feel his ache there, knew he saw a cruise or retirement or paradise in the picture he'd chosen. Lolo saw sharks and drownings and Dengue fever. She saw death. She always saw death.

She opened a spreadsheet, maximizing the window so columns of numbers overtook her screen. Order. She didn't ever tell Manny that she didn't like the backgrounds, never changed them to something more comforting. "Do you think Henry and that girl, the redhead? You think they got something going?" she said. He was on the bed behind her, reading a spy novel. Escaping.

"Maybe."

Lolo wanted to point out the threat the girl could pose. The danger. But it was sometimes hard to gauge her responses to things—was she being melodramatic? Paranoid? So she said, "She's married, I think."

"Maybe."

Manny didn't believe his brother Henry's business was any of their business. "He lets us live here, baby," he'd say to Lolo whenever she bitched about Henry. "Give the guy some space," he'd say.

They paid rent, though. Not a lot when they moved in, it's true, but more every month as she made more. As the business she'd built for the three of them—that she'd damn well invented—took off. And Henry brought all his trouble to the house with him. Ridiculous parties she had to hide from. Married girls and their pissed off husbands. His loud friends so eager to show off their strength they wrestled right through the furniture, breaking anything not hidden away.

She didn't turn to face her husband. "You don't think that this is a bad idea?" she said. "I mean we can't have her just hanging out around here, seeing everything."

For once, Manny didn't shut her down. "I'll talk to him."

The bit of fenced yard behind Henry's wood frame house, so cloaked and shaded by twin oaks and pines that it almost felt like being inside, was one of the only outside spaces Lolo could still handle. She pulled a pack of Marlboro Reds from behind the Blessed Virgin's halo. She had to squat in the overgrown grass to ferret her lighter out of the nook where Mary's wimple met her gown, below her ear and behind the crest of her shoulder, the molded concrete cool and rough in the hollow there. She kissed the Virgin square on the head and pushed out of her squat, bending as if the arch of the sky loomed too low. "Momma, excuse my French," she said to the Mary, "but these needy cunts are going to be the death of me." She lit her cigarette and said a prayer, her eye on the house.

There were three women in there. The redhead and two others. They were the sort that, in high school, Lolo would have called the pretty girls. Hair perfectly messy in sporty topknots, jeans that looked tailored to dip and slouch around their curves, and white skin, tanned to a crisp, dark-but-not-too-dark gold. She didn't even know Red's name, the others were—no, she didn't know any of their names. In her head, they were all Jane: Fat Jane, Red Jane, and Smells like Onions Jane. The kitchen was so crowded the air became heavy, warm and damp and smothering, everyone's breath on her. Three women, her husband, his good for nothing brother, her little mutt Port (barking and coughing and carrying on in what sounded more like death throes than aggression), and five little Igloo coolers of donated breast milk.

Smells like Onions was a champion pumper. Two of those coolers were hers.

"Lolo? Did you find some?"

Lolo put the cigarette out on the bottom of her shoe and tossed it in the lilies edging her neighbor's ditch. What her husband Manny meant was, "Lolo, stop screwing around and get in here." He knew better than to say it, the way he knew better than to ask if she'd been smoking again, but after fifteen years, he didn't need to.

In her pocket was the "some" of what she'd offered to go forage for the women, their squawking sending her looking for an excuse to visit the Virgin and her Marlboros. She'd picked nothing more exciting than a handful of dandelion leaves that she passed off as blessed thistle—for milk production. God, they loved magic herbs. She neither had the thistle nor fully trusted its safety as far as their babies were concerned, and she drew a line there. Whenever they came, she picked the dandelions from the closest edge of the ditch, wild and unruly thanks to a dispute with the landlord, and told the Janes to add just a few leaves to a salad, "really just a tiny few each meal."

At least they'd eat some vegetables.

Inside, Lolo affected an accent. Above her own faint southern roll, she folded a Hispanic lilt somewhere in between her Tia Espie's and one she remembered from a psychic commercial that played constantly when she was a child in Miami. Not a strong accent, just something a little more exotic than small town Louisiana generally got. "I found some," she said. "Not a lot. You will have to share." She draped the leaves across the counter as solemnly as she could. When she was little, her grandmother had draped rosaries she brought in from trips to South America and Europe in just the same way, the gesture gentle, her back bent as if in a bow. "My mama, god rest her—"

Manny coughed. It sounded a lot like he said "Jesus." Lolo didn't bother to shoot him a look. He knew better.

"She believed it was best to pick everything under a full moon." Lolo made a show of looking heavenward as if she could see either the moon or her mother (who was currently draped across a lounge chair on a half-priced cruise to Jamaica) through the popcorn ceiling in the rental. Then she laughed, a chicken noise so loud it startled poor Port, who took to wheezing. "But I don't think the plants are that picky. All right, ladies. You know the drill. Put it in your salad only."

Port jumped on Henry's lap and coughed out a look-at-me bark. Henry was making eyes at Red Jane instead of putting the breast milk in the fridge, and Lolo liked to believe Port was telling him to get off his ass, doing his duty as her loyal dog. In truth, he liked Henry, who roughhoused with him and took him on rides in the truck, better than he liked her. Everyone did.

Lolo checked Red Jane. Sure enough, she was making googly eyes right back at Henry. Like a fucking teenager.

Lolo crossed the kitchen in order to put her hand on Red's shoulder, to turn the woman's attention away from Henry, out the door, and on to her Mommy's Night Out drinks with her little friends, but the room was so small she knocked into Fat Jane before she made it to Red. "Fuck," Lolo said, "Sorry, momma." Before Manny was laid off, she'd had a nice kitchen with tile counters and enough room to make a Thanksgiving meal. It was a kitchen you could maneuver around without touching anyone, ever.

Fat Jane planted her hands, hands that were always touching her mouth, her nose, touching everything, on Lolo as if to steady herself. She was a dramatic woman. On more than one occasion, Lolo had seen her kiss her fingers and touch the bags she dropped off. "For the orphans," Fat Jane would say, her voice dropping at the end as she pressed her just kissed fingers to the bags while Henry unloaded them from her Igloo. She loved to use the word "orphan," saying it two or three times a visit in a quiet whisper, the way other people said "cancer." Now, she leaned in for a bear hug. "You're doing God's work," she said. Lolo tried her best to relax into the other woman's bosom, to not turn rigid or recoil from the embrace she already knew would linger too long. At least Fat Jane always smelled good, like expensive perfume applied lightly, a bit of jasmine on top of the smell of baby powder and Desitin that circled the room when the women came with their coolers.

"No, it is you three," Lolo said, finally wriggling free. "You are the ones donating. The ones doing His work."

Lolo slid out of the button-up she'd put on to meet with the Janes, leaving it splayed on the floor, still buttoned. Her arms itched from the fabric touching her, itched from Fat Jane touching her, itched from the breath of all the Janes touching her, from the way they all felt the need to lay a hand on her arm or shoulder or wrist as they said goodbye, the now empty Igloos swinging in their grips. Saint Lolo, patron of hungry, baby orphans everywhere. The tank top she wore underneath, like most of her others, was ripped, but she couldn't stand the idea of going out to the store to try on new ones, and she'd put on some weight, wasn't sure what size to order. She just kept wearing the ones she had.

"Manny, where'd you put the box from Amazon?" she called out, slipping her shoes off as Port danced around her feet. "And bring me those cut-offs on the bed, huh?" She took off her pants and Port snuggled into her pile of discarded clothes. "Now you love me," she said to the dog. The affected accent was gone, leaving only a bit of a drawl that just barely smudged and smeared the edges of her words. "Do you see them?" she said, once again raising her voice so Manny could hear her in the next room. "They might be on the floor there. Manny, are you listening to me? And look, tell Henry, I'll have these ready to take out to the freezer in a bit. I ain't waiting for him to save his game." The men had turned on the PlayStation the second the Janes disappeared.

"Henry can hear you. Everyone in the neighborhood can hear you, chica."

The breast milk that Henry'd emptied from the coolers was stacked in a messy pile in the fridge. She got all but three bags out. Each of the Janes used the same standing storage bags. Lolo'd shown the women where to buy them online the first time she had the group over, and they were very good about buying just what she asked. They were her best girls.

A nun from Saint Jerome's Children's Home would come pick up about a third of the bags that women like the Janes donated. The rest went with Manny and Henry to the weightlifters, football players, and wannabes they sold to in the parking lots and locker rooms of local gyms.

She found her life was easiest if she recruited pumpers in numbers, little groups of friends that shuffled in and out together, that saw each other's coolers, noticed each other's output. And she aimed for women just like the Janes. Pretty, middle class girls who searched for books about organic composting and baby sign language online. She found them through her tech support job. Everything was automated by a neat little program she coded. Whenever someone fit the shopping profile she set up and also lived within a hundred-mile radius, the program noticed. The data was shuffled along to a print on demand site and the woman was sent glossy pamphlets about the hungry orphans at Saint Jerome's. Manny had done a good job designing the brochures, clean lines, a fancy logo.

He was so good it broke her heart. He missed working. She knew it.

When a breastfeeding woman with more than enough milk to donate read Manny's pamphlet and, tears choking her as she imagined the hollow stomachs plaguing a clutch of motherless babes, called Lolo, Lolo encouraged her to connect with like-minded pals before setting up an informational get together. "The more the merrier," she'd say, her voice as bright as she could make it.

Manny dropped the cardboard box she'd asked for on the counter and kissed her. "You're going to feel like shit if something happens to Mama H after you've been telling people she's dead."

"I ain't said she was dead."

He popped her on the butt, just where the leg of her underwear cut her soft fat, and Lolo squeaked, happy to pretend to be silly and young. "All right, all right. I sort of did, but you have to admit it was funny."

He gave her another kiss and nodded. "There's more than enough milk in the back freezer to do a delivery," he said.

"This set will round out another case, plus some. You and Henry can circle around to the gyms with them tomorrow."

Writing the original program was just a distraction, a fun data mining project that stretched her mind better than what she did all day, suggesting customers turn computers off and on again when the company site locked up. Lolo liked doing back-end work, hated customers, actually, but they mostly gave those assignments to the guys who would—who could—go into the office. So she'd started mining data as a side project. The breast milk came later, after she heard one of Henry's jock friends brag about its benefits. He got it directly from the source, apparently, and claimed right boobs were better than lefts.

Lolo cut open the box and pulled out the bag of caffeine powder she'd ordered. Ten years ago, when she stopped leaving the house, their old house, their real house, shopping wasn't this easy. Manny had to do everything for them then, work, groceries, bills, everything. She pulled a couple of trays filled with plastic capped tubes from the cabinet. She ordered those online, too. Each held less than three ounces, a perfect shot for a big man, and was freezable. "Hey, where's my scale?" she said. She looked past Manny to the living room. "Damn it, Henry, do you have the scale?"

"Hold on," he called back. "Manny, you should see this shit. I'm killing it."

"Henry, I swear to God— No, asshole, I swear to the Virgin that if I have to come in there and take my fucking scale from you again I will put a knife through your pretty abs."

"Come get some, puta."

Manny made a show of rolling his eyes as Lolo pantomimed knifing the both of them. "You people need to calm your tits. It's ok, bro, I'll come get it," he said.

The caffeine had to be measured carefully. Lolo weighed each spoonful before whisking it into the milk. It took very little over the maximum dosage to do real damage, maybe even kill a person. And caffeine powder was bitter as hell. Putting a small enough amount in the milk so that the taste was masked while simultaneously getting in a large enough dose to give a little kick was a matter of precision and care, the key to convincing their clients breast milk did everything Manny and Henry and the internet message boards promised. Everything their little hearts desired. Make them stronger. Faster. Have more stamina. Increase muscle density. Cure fucking cancer. Walk on water. All without shrinking their balls. The caffeine powder provided the unexpected zing any skeptics needed. And it was cheap. And legal to buy.

The whole enterprise was basically legal. Mostly legal. And nearly 100% profit.

Lolo poured and capped, poured and capped until her little linoleum counter was covered in line after line of individually bottled breast milk shots. An army of money making soldiers that would free her and Manny and Port from his brother's shitty little rental house and get them back to as near a normal life as Lolo could manage.

The headset Lolo wore to do customer support was too tight under her ear, prickling a pressure point, but it was the cheapest bluetooth set she could find and it freed her to wander the yard with Port.

"Yes. Yes. Right. I will, absolutely. But I need you to tell me exactly what the error message says." Her cigarettes were a bit damp with morning dew and she imagined mold spores flecking the tobacco, blooming in her lungs, spreading like clover until she was a mess of fluffed up white and green inside. "No, sir." With a little effort, she lit one anyway. "Yes, sir. But to help you I really need the exact message, sir." She closed her eyes and filled the air with smoke rings while the gentleman on the other end of the line yelled at her. She didn't watch them rise into the big empty sky, a thing to panic under, but enjoyed the act, the way the memory of learning to puff them out seemed to have settled into her muscles more than her mind.

She sat down next to Mary, pulled an oversized phone from her back pocket, and using her pinky, remoted into her computer and then into the customer's. "Ok, sir," she leaned her head against the statue's shoulder, "can you show me exactly what you were doing when the error message appeared?"

The sound of Manny's truck, coughing and grumbling out of gear, and then Port, coughing and grumbling into gear as he barked out his greeting, drowned out the beginning of the client's answer. But he was yelling again anyways, so Lolo just nodded her head against the folds of the Virgin's veil and smoked.

When the nun from Saint Jerome's knocked, her signature 'shave and a haircut' pounding, Lolo had to answer the door. Henry was screwing Red Jane in the backroom and Manny was delivering a crate of breast shots to a high school coach with a big game on the horizon. It was the sort of situation that made Lolo itch. All of it was horrible.

The nun trying to make small talk.

Red Jane's grunting.

Port answering each and every guttural groan with a wheezing cough.

Lolo's own quick breaths as her anxiety mounted.

It was a symphony of horrible. And the fear that Red Jane would appear, half naked and sweaty, and see how just little of her milk the nun left with, would find out exactly what they were up to, was just icing on the shit cake.

This was Manny's job, this nun stuff, and Lolo scratched deep grooves in her arms until the nun was gone, swinging two grocery bags of frozen breast milk and cold packs out the door and to the children's home. At least she hadn't been wearing a wimple.

Lolo hid in the yard, leaning against the Virgin until Red Jane was also gone and Manny was home. "I hate him," she said to Manny as he rubbed his hands over the welts on her arms.

"I know. But he loves you. He loves me. He loves Port. And, besides, you hate everyone." He pinched her side to make her laugh and Lolo did, happy to at least pretend.

Since the nun, she'd mostly hidden in the bedroom, the rest of the house feeling less hers than usual. Even the kitchen was lost to her. A strange space. She left anything she couldn't take care of from the bed to the boys.

"I need you to turn on desktop sharing," Lolo said. She picked a thread from the bedspread and tried to imagine a face for the man on the other end of the call. But she wasn't good with faces, even in her imagination. "There should be a little square you can check, mm hmmm, uh huh. Sir? Sir? Sir, is your computer on?"

She could hear Henry banging around in the kitchen. Messing up all of her careful order. Her fridge, her freezer, she knew they would be a jumbled mess now.

The boys were just not clean and careful like she was. She had to do everything.

A woman's voice climbed over the clamor occasionally. Lolo slid under the covers.

And though she still slipped outside with Port in the early mornings, keeping her eyes low so she could imagine the little fence line stretched high enough to keep her safe from the outside world, the trips were getting shorter, her imagination filling the tight yard with a misty sense of danger.

The sun had barely crested the fence the morning Henry came running out of the house so fast that Lolo ducked, terrified he was going to bowl her over.

She had, by now, stopped going further from the house then the first tree, a fat, old Sawtooth Oak she thought of as homebase. She had Manny move The Virgin under its thick branches. Ducking Henry sent her nearly out of its shadow. Dangerously so.

Her throat felt tight.

She pressed the mute button next to her ear. "What are you doing awake?" She knew it sounded like "I hate you," but couldn't stop herself. He'd ruined it. Ruined the last bit of outside and now she was trapped in it, him between her and the door.

"Chel took the wrong milk," he said.

"What?"

"She isn't answering her cell."

"Who?" Lolo un-pressed the mute button. "Sir, I think we are having connectivity issues. I can't quite hear—" She tapped the button twice more, cutting herself off and hanging up the phone. Removed the headset. "Who took what wrong milk?" Even in the sheltered shadow of the tree, she could feel the delicious, calming heat of the sun breaking through the branches. Instead of looking up to catch sight of the shifting light, she tried to follow its movements in the shadows on the ground behind Henry.

He put his hand over his face. "Late last night, we had some champagne to celebrate her divorce papers. You know how she is, she didn't want to risk any of it—"

"Who is?"

"Chel. She was going to pump and dump once she got home, but needed some milk for this morning's feeding in case her ex used all she left with him. I told her to grab some from the fridge."

Confused, Lolo just looked at Henry.

"God dammit, niña, listen. Chel. My girlfriend. Two months. Red hair. How the fuck do you not know this?"

Lolo brushed her nails across her skin. She had no answer. But she understood now.

Red. She took the wrong milk. To her infant.

She wanted to leave the yard. To get back in the house. Her bedroom. She wanted to lie down and nap until Manny got home. She wanted to switch the direction of the conversation away from her, what she missed, wanted to chastise him for being careless. Why was the caffeinated milk in the front fridge to begin with, she wanted to say, why the fuck hadn't he put everything in its place, used her neat, clean layout, her careful rows? But the panic on his face stopped her. "Are you sure? Are you a hundred percent positive?"

"I don't know. Yes. Probably. Maybe." Lolo could hear Henry's teeth clattering together as he thought, a habit he'd had for as long as she'd known him. "I don't know. You told us not to store them next to each other. You were, you know, sleeping a lot, and it just seemed faster. I can't—"

This wasn't her fault.

How could she have known? Lolo shifted down into the grass and said the words silently. Not my fault. "Okay. You have to get her. It's that simple. You and Manny. You have to go get her before she feeds the baby. How old is it?"

Manny. She needed Manny.

"Six months. And I can't go. Manny has the truck. He's out getting groceries."

"You have to call her."

"I told you—"

Lolo hid her shaking hands. "Then call him." Why wasn't he here with her?

When she still watched TV, she'd liked cop shows, nature shows, mysteries, documentaries. They'd watched a lot together, on the couch, bodies touching easily, no work to it. Even as she slowly stopped leaving the house, at first just afraid to drive, then to ride, then to be in crowded places, then in open places, in those first couple of years she'd let the outside world in through her television. But finally, that stopped, too. She'd been very careful to keep everything out. Keep herself safe. Sharks, Drownings, Dengue, Murderers, Parasites, Falling, Fires, Crowds, Heights, Careening Accidents, Collapsing Buildings, she'd spent ten years imagining every possible dangerous, terrifying thing. Real things, fake things. She'd taken up less and less space. They both had.

"He isn't picking up."

In all these years, Lolo'd never once imagined she was the danger. The thing someone else would need protecting from.

"Call 911," she said. "If you can't get Red—Chel—if you really can't get her, we have to call 911."

Nothing they'd done had been legal. No matter what she told herself, what she told Manny, what she whispered to the Mary on her smoke breaks, it hadn't been. And it was all her idea. Her fault.

She could not stand anymore. Sat in the grass in front of the Virgin. Leaned her head as far back as it would go, the concrete behind her a comforting stop, and tried to open her eyes. She tried to force herself to look into the dizzying blue above.

Without changing position, she pressed the keys on her handset. She didn't need to look to find them.

"What's your emergency?"

She wanted to say, "I need Manny," but of course she didn't. That would be insane. She tried to concentrate on the baby. That she'd hurt the baby if she didn't speak. That suddenly she was filled with horrible power. But it was hard. She pressed her head further back, so a sharp edge in the statue's concrete grated against her scalp and wondered what prison would be like. Everything dirty. Everything touching.

Alone. And never alone.

Lolo strained to hear the truck, to hear Port greeting her husband.

As if she could will Manny into being the way she tried to will the rest of the world away.

Her closed lids burned orange, and as she found the words, Lolo imagined falling upward, disappearing into the overwhelming space she knew was there waiting.

"Patchwork Identity" by Kelsey Bryan-Zwick

MAKING CHALLAH WHILE HEARING OF RBG'S DEATH

by Babo Kamel

As from a tunnel, someone wails a loud
long *no*. Then *no, no, no no*. But there is
no tunnel. Only you. Erev Rosh Hashana
hands deep in batter and the air turns sour.

You miss your mother's wooden bowl
her Blue Onion plates, her simple kitchen
the dishwasher's slow hum, the linoleum.
You knead the dough, knead and knead

until it forms a soft ball you cover
with a tea towel, black striped as a prayer
shawl men would wear and finally women
too, the Torah equally theirs.

For two hours the bread rises as promised
You punch it down with closed fists. You do
this for her and all the chain of Ruths who,
pounded down, must rise and rise again.

♥☙♥

IS THIS A JOKE?
by Leslie Pietrzyk

Nothing you own matches—blouses don't go with pantsuits; skirts don't match up with sweaters. Not one thing in this entire walk-in closet of shelves and bins and racks and hangers and drawers composes a wearable outfit.

You're awfully dramatic. Mathematically and aesthetically, there are many dozen outfits here. But right now, standing here in your room in your robe and unable to commit to the right bra, the right shapewear, one designer, not even skirt vs. dress, pantsuit vs. skirt, black vs. navy vs. floral vs. colorblock...nothing matches, nothing is right, and, truly, there's nothing to wear.

Sure, any number of homeless women or even middle-class women would gobble up ten seconds of access to your closet, scooping great clattery chunks of anything on a hanger, shrieking with immense glee, "Boo-hoo to your first world problems! Boo-fucking-hoo!" You don't expect sympathy for this particular problem, or any of your problems, really.

So. How to solve a problem no one cares about?

This morning he said, "Wear something hot tonight." But he kept talking: "Wear something that doesn't make you look—"

Your eyes darted up from their hazy examination of the coffee. You set down the mug, fidgeted it into a pleasing alignment then studied the picture of a Ferris wheel on this mug that was purchased two years ago at the State Fair of Texas for fifteen dollars. You considered, briefly, the benefits of strolling out of the kitchen, of leaving behind this question. You asked it: "Doesn't what?"

He heaved out a vast sigh. His turn to stare blankly at a meaningless whatever, and he seemed to choose to gaze upon the professionally maintained lawn through the sliding glass door, ornamented with a koi pond, fire pit, brick barbecue, and artful shrubbery and annuals, perfectly irrigated through this period of no rain. Surely he knows that lodged in your head is a perpetual to-do list of service and maintenance appointments, of names and phone numbers, of how and when and where and why and what is needed for modern life to function, indeed, for all things to function: pool, drycleaning, housecleaning, car detailing, groceries, regular laundry, holiday catering menus, annual HVAC check-ups, which plumber comes after-hours, appliance repair, where the extra batteries are, why there's always enough toilet paper and paper towels, a plastic bin of emergency storm/terrorist attack/zombie apocalypse supplies, leftover solar eclipse glasses from 2017, holiday card list, stamps, bills to pay, receipts to file, software to update, and on. Surely he knows the extent of everything you *do*, every detail stuffed inside your head, oozing into every last scrap of brain.

Right? "Doesn't what?" you asked. "Make me look old?" you asked. "Doesn't make me look old?" you asked a second time, then locking it in in case of confusion. "I should wear something tonight that doesn't make me look old?"

"I never said that," he said.

You only thought it, was your silent zinger.

Back to your closet with all its clothes, the clothes that make you look old.

You stare into it for a long time, maybe pondering a not necessarily unexpected future. But you still get hit on. Men of all ages whip their heads around to watch you walk. At parties women side-eye as their husbands and boyfriends net you into their conversations. These things happen TO YOU, ALL THE TIME.

You gently slide shut the pocket doors of this pretty closet—professionally organized as are all the closets, including his, another project you supervised. Put a dollar figure on all these clothes and maybe he'd like them more. Tell him which stores, which designers, show dog-eared magazines and YouTube red carpets that feature that dress and those shoes, and reel through the numbers as you talk and talk and talk, proving yourself beautiful. (Proving your worth.) Watch him then drop to his knees, begging you to believe that now he understands how pretty you are, how beautiful, how his beloved wife is hot, hott, hawt, sexy, smoking, stunning, gorgeous, drop-dead, deer-in-the-headlights, pow-zow-woweee! "I love you," he might conclude. "Just the way you are. Forever."

But here's the truth: you're a body covered by clothes. In the end, the clothes have nothing to do with any of it. Your body. Your worth. Your value.

You.

Some would say, kindly or un-, that this is about what you deserve.

You stand. You think. And you think. And when the thinking is done, you tighten the sash of your robe into a hard, solid knot. You walk downstairs, barefoot—even the slippers in the closet disgust you—and you perch on one of the teak stools at the kitchen island. There's coffee in the pot, cold and leftover from this morning, and you pour some into a mug with a picture of a panda. You jump up and pull the Texas Ferris wheel mug out of the dishwasher and drop it into the garbage. Such a satisfying thunk as it hits the bottom. This panda mug is ugly—pandas aren't even your thing—so you chuck it. The cupboard holds a shelf of way too many mugs from trips you've taken with him, mugs marking the years of this marriage. A clutter of time, ticking away thirty to forty to death. That hotel in Yosemite, that trip to Paris, that weekend at the Broadmoor, London, New York, Nantucket. You'll tell the housekeeper to throw away every single mug, and online you'll order timeless white porcelain bistro mugs, each with the exact same sleek, clean lines.

Oh my god. It's a plan.

You sit back down on the teak stool and wait.

He appears, wearing his dinner-downtown uniform: John Varvatos sport jacket and Loro Piana pants tailored to that annoying signature 1 ¾ inch cuff, custom shirt, sockless Ferragamo loafers, and a gold bordered silk pocket square the Barney's girl in Vegas picked out for him that you happen to know is Gucci.

"Happy birthday," you say, and as you tiptoe up, he tilts down for a cheek kiss.

"Six-oh," he says. "Jesus Christ." But unrattled. Undaunted. His face is comfortable, with a nice celebrity scruff happening—not too gray, not too obviously colored—gel-tamed eyebrows, which you taught him to do. A few faint squint lines, the kind that sea captains and bowl-winning coaches have: men of vision, leaders, men in command of manly men. You try to be clinical in your appraisal, but it's just different with men, isn't it? He's solidly good-looking.

He's rich.

He's someone who was someone on the football field and still is, a little bit, enough to get good tables and good service, to buy his way in on that or his money. You sigh inside, but keep it small.

He says, "Thought you said we were leaving at six-thirty?"

You glance at the place where the Cartier tank usually goes, but your wrist is deliciously empty. "Yes, six-thirty."

"It's six-thirty-five," he says.

"So you're a teensy bit late," you say with a nice, natural, non-accusatory smile. "The birthday boy gets to do what he wants." Which is oopsily dangerous to say, because then he turns hopeful and says:

"Are we—?"

"No." You're firm. This is not about that.

My god. You're so exhausted.

"But—" The word dangles as he gives a long up and down. You stand, presenting the full view. The robe's lined in heavy white terrycloth with a faux polished silkiness as the outside layer. You liked wearing it in a hotel the two of you stayed at last year so he popped it into the suitcase, saying no one would actually charge for it, which they didn't. The resort name is tastefully embroidered in white thread above your left breast. At the moment, there's a mug in the cupboard with that same logo.

"You're absolutely right," you say. "I need shoes," and you walk over to the sliding glass door and finagle your bare feet into a pair of dull green, plastic gardening clogs that you wear when watering the patio herbs and flowerboxes. "Now I'm ready," you announce. "Time to go."

He circles a complete 360, utterly confused. Pats his pockets for sunglasses, phone, keys. This is how well you know him, that he's so disciplined that when you say, I'm ready, he is ready.

Then he says, "It was hard getting that reservation."

"I hear the Dover sole is exquisite," I say.

"But you're not going? Headache on my birthday?"

Maybe he doesn't intend to sound like a child, but he does. I say, "I'm going. And *yes*, I'm ready. *Let's go.*"

"You can't wear *that*," he says.

"Put something on," he says.

"That red dress," he says. "I like that one."

"The black one," he says.

"You have at least two hundred dresses, don't you?" he says.

"Come on," he says.

"Jesus fucking Christ," he says.

"We're going to be late," he says.

"You hate being late," he says.

"You're always on me for being late," he says.

"What is this?" he says.

Finally he says, "This is a joke."

You unknot the robe sash, slide the sleeves down your arms, letting the garment puddle to the floor. Here's your body, you think, your lotioned, loofahed, massaged, yogaed, low-carbed, no glutened, sugar-denied, Slim-Fasted, Lean Cuisined, Ketoed, Atkinsed, weight-trained, SoulCycled, Pelotoned, carved, sculpted, surgeried, nipped and tucked, lipoed, old body. There you are.

"This is no joke," you say. "Look at me."

And there you are, there you are: what you have made yourself into. What you were all along.

"Ready for the best birthday ever?" you say, dazzling the smile that charmed him once. "*Let's go.*"

❧❦❧

REGARDING THAT PACKAGE
by Wendy Besel Hahn

May 28, 2019
Justice Kavanaugh
The Supreme Court of the United States
One First Street N.E.
Washington, D.C., 20543

Dear Hon. Justice Brett Kavanaugh,

If you or your clerk is reading this, I trust my package cleared the mail-room. I imagine the handlers in suits using radiation on the package to neutralize the glass jar filled with formaldehyde and human tissue. I assure you such protocol was a futile exercise: my mother's uterine sarcoma survived all previous medical attempts to shrink it prior to its removal. Please consider the specimen a token of my disapproval concerning your decision to let Mike Pence's absurd legislation stand.

Last week I brought my twelve-year-old daughter to the steps of the Supreme Court to protest, but you refused to hear appeals to Indiana's law forcing women to bury or cremate fetal remains after miscarriages and abortions. I never would have thought of sending this piece of Mom, but the coroner had said the mass in her uterus was about "the size of a mango" when he removed it. As someone who uses common fruits to help pregnant women visualize their fetuses, I couldn't dismiss the parallel. I hope you keep the specimen in your chambers to remind you of the importance of reproductive healthcare.

As a fellow Catholic, I get your antiabortion leaning. I've also read you have marked Matthew 25 in your office Bible. That gives me hope that you might consider the women I see in my Arlington women's clinic—the ones who don't have money for birth control and who rely on food stamps to feed their kids—as part of the "least among us" whom you've vowed to serve.

I didn't send a picture of my own daughter; I figure you have two of your own. I'm curious what you tell them about consent and about their maturing bodies. I hope they never have to treat a patient like the immigrant woman from El Salvador who was so desperate to avoid another baby that she destroyed her own womb with a metal knitting needle.

Lest you discount my letter as the ranting of a wayward Catholic nurse, I want you to know I held my mother's hand on her deathbed as the tumor ate away her insides. I recited "Hail Mary" so many times through tears that my mind mixed up "Fruit of thy womb" with "Fruit of thy tomb." During her funeral mass at Our Lady Queen of Peace Catholic Church, I eulogized her while I stood underneath a portrait of the Black Madonna in front of the patients I've treated throughout my career.

I want you to know there is more than one way to be a Catholic.

Sincerely,
Emma Kowalski, NP

WAREHOUSE SALE
by Cecilia Baader

She'd stuck him in a Barneys bag. It was the first one I'd seen up close. Absurd: a shopping bag nicer than the purse I carried, though that wasn't difficult.

He'd have hated it. Or laughed, then resented it later.

"You know you can sell those now on eBay," I said, startling a laugh out of her.

"I didn't know what else to do," Lisa confessed, standing cooly with the black bag nestled between her feet. She was tiny and sleek, a younger Anna Wintour. She was wearing a denim jacket, but she wasn't sweating.

"Barneys bags," I said. "People still like them. More so now that they're rare."

She considered the bag at her feet. "I don't blame them. It's the only bag I could find with strong enough handles."

She grimaced when she caught me lingering on the bag. "They might have wanted him right away, and I didn't want to make this trip twice." Honestly, I had to give her credit for getting this far. Lisa never left the city if she could help it.

I didn't tell her it was odd because one of the last things Paul had asked of me was to be kind to her. It wasn't her fault that she didn't love him, he'd said. So I promised, mostly because I never thought I'd actually be held to it.

I tried, I really did, but I was a mess. My sandals stuck to the ground. I wore a sleeveless shirt, probably too informal for the occasion—I surreptitiously checked my armpits, but they were still dry. It felt like Sorority Rush all over again.

I wasn't picked then, either.

A teenage busker in a durag set up with a worn plastic work bucket on the platform nearby, and we wordlessly moved away. He started playing and his buddy started doing tricks on a BMX bike. It was impressive, but everyone ignored them. Except Lisa: "Why are they here?" she asked. "It's not like this is where the tourists are."

"Probably on their way home," I replied. "Can't spend all day in Times Square."

We found a spot further down the platform and she settled the Barneys Bag between her feet again. I wanted to tell her not to put him on the ground, but the boy started drumming again and drowned me out. Also, what could I say? He wasn't my husband.

"What?" She caught my look and shrugged. "He's heavy," she said. "And anyway, I double-bagged him."

I kept staring at the bag. "Do you want to see?" she asked.

"No," I said. Then, "Yes."

She picked it up and I peered inside. Honestly, the bag was nicer than the box. They'd put his ashes in a cheap plastic box. It was ivory and ribbed for her pleasure.

She was going to put him on the ground again, so I told her I would carry the bag. She hadn't lied: he *was* heavy.

The R Train finally arrived, and we got on. The bucket kid got on the next car down.

Stand Clear of the Closing Doors, Please, the train announced. The bike trickster jostled me as he launched himself through the opening. The door caught his wheel and we were delayed. Shamelessly he sprinted down the center aisle to the next car while I caught my balance.

Lisa reached out and steadied me.

The last time I saw Paul was our best day. We met in Brooklyn instead of the city like usual because I wanted to set eyes on him before I left. It wasn't often that we were both fine, though he was complaining of headaches. They were always getting his meds wrong and the weeks following each doctor's visit felt like a science experiment.

He'd grown up in Park Slope back when it was more of a working-class neighborhood. I gave him an excuse to come home, and he paid me back by pointing at landmarks as we walked and telling me forgotten scandals. I was fascinated by the story of the baby's bones they'd found inside a wall while renovating a brownstone on President Street and kept making him give me more details. "What do you think happened?" I whispered. I tried not to delight, but I loved learning these secrets for the same reason I listened to true crime podcasts.

"I think someone had a baby they weren't supposed to have, and they hid the evidence," he said.

Was it a miscarriage? Murder? A stillbirth? I considered a moment. I didn't know if that made it better or worse. "Am I too ghoulish?" I asked.

Paul shrugged when I asked his opinion. "Either way, it was a hundred years ago," he said. "Nobody to ask now."

I eyeballed the next brownstone. "What's in the walls of that one?" I wondered aloud.

"Rats," Paul said.

We turned down Seventh Avenue toward Flatbush, and he pointed out the site of the Seventh Avenue plane crash. I hadn't realized it happened right around the corner from my apartment. Paul pointed out the damage, and I bent down to study the burn marks on the corner of a building. I don't know what I was looking for. It's not like there would be blood stains. "How old were you when it crashed?" I asked, brushing my fingers on the stone.

"Oh," he said, inspecting his scuffed brown shoes. "I wasn't born yet."

You'd never know it happened except that people didn't want you to forget. One guy still had newspaper clippings posted in his shop window. A lesser plane crash, one that had already faded into memory.

Paul peered over my shoulder to read the article. "Sounds about right." It would have killed his Uncle Scottie, except he got lucky. "He worked at some church as a handyman, but he wasn't at work that day."

"Where was he?"

"Drinking with my Dad," he said. "They liked to start early." He laughed, but didn't add anything further. He didn't need to. I'd heard all about his dad.

Paul took my elbow and I let him, leaning into him comfortably. We walked down Seventh past a little bodega where I liked to buy my breakfast. The guy in there didn't know my name, but he knew my order. I didn't know his name, either, but I liked his fresh flowers and fruit. He had a brother who had a cart right by the Q train and between them, they had more variety than I'd seen in my whole grocery store back home. "You know," I said. "I'd never even seen a plantain before I moved here."

"We can't all be eating cheese."

I shook my head. "I give up on you."

"No," he said. "Don't. Ever. You're the only thing that keeps me going."

I was shocked by his ferocity and took a step back. A bicyclist whizzed by and he pulled me out of danger. "Cheezus," I said, and he nearly lost his shit laughing over that one, and briefly, we were normal again.

Once, before I decided to go to grad school in New York, I'd brought my ex-boyfriend Miles to meet him. We were on again at the time. I'd engineered the whole trip just to see Paul, but I figured if Miles came too, it wouldn't look suspicious. Miles wasn't stupid, though, and immediately hated Paul.

Lisa sensed it, and the two of us banded together to rescue the evening. She knew this place in the Village that had been featured on some show I hadn't seen, but the pizza was no great shakes.

The waiter came by to check on us after the food arrived.

"Good grief," said Paul. "You can't even fold it." He was a purist about these things, and Miles pounced.

"Pizza shouldn't have to be folded to be good," announced Miles.

Lisa ordered another round of drinks. She was right. We weren't drunk enough.

The silence stretched while we waited, so I launched into a story about how Miles was late for our flight but I got on the plane anyway because he wasn't answering his phone. I spent the entire flight fuming, and then when I got off the plane, his phone went straight to voicemail.

"That's because I was running," he said.

"Sounds cinematic," said Lisa. "Did you have to leap over luggage carts?"

I scoffed. "Him?"

"I leap," said Miles. "I'm a leaper."

Paul pulled out his phone and started to scroll idly. "So did you make the plane?"

"I made the next one," Miles said, a hint of red on his neck.

"What happened?" asked Paul. "Did you kick over someone's calfskin luggage and they had to detain you?"

"Something like that," Miles said. He was flaming red now.

I rolled my eyes. "He was in Prague and missed the connecting flight."

"I love Prague," said Lisa. "It's the next best thing to Paris. Flowers everywhere. Shops, carts, hillsides." She shared a long look with Paul. "You could fill a whole hotel room with flowers."

"You could," said Paul, typing on his phone.

"It's almost better than Paris, even." She touched his knee.

Paul looked up from his phone finally. "Sure," he said. "Almost."

My phone chirped. *I'm sorry,* said Paul's text. *We had a fight before we got here. She's feeling insecure.*

Same, I texted back.

"Almost only counts in hand grenades and horseshoes," I said aloud. "Did I mention I saw our Broadway show all alone?" It was this weird show called *Metamorphoses,* and it was like nothing I'd ever seen. The actors played in and around a swimming pool and for the first time ever, Orpheus and Eurydice brought me to tears. Nobody else had seen it and I trailed off lamely. "I've never seen anything like it," I said.

"That sounds really good," said Lisa. "Maybe you and I could go to see something sometime. Paul never wants to go with me to the theater."

"You know how Orpheus died?" asked Paul. "He wandered around singing about his lost love and sang so beautifully that the women tore him to pieces and threw him in the River Styx."

"I can relate," said Miles.

"Listen, my dismembering days are over," I said. Then, "I'll forgive you if you ask."

"I got on the next plane," said Miles. He looked to me for moral support, but I wasn't interested in giving it. "Also, you could have waited too."

"I'm flabbergasted," I said. "Watch the gas, how it lights."

He started to say something, then muttered, "You are a deeply unserious person."

"What are you talking about?" I said. "I'm a goddamn delight."

Lisa elbowed Paul in the ribs. "On one thing we can agree," Paul announced, "Broadway is overrated."

"No it's not," Lisa and I said together. We all laughed too loudly, and someone looking at us from the outside would have thought we were friends.

The waiter finally brought our drinks. Lisa clinked her glass with Miles and started comparing notes on Prague. She worked in an art gallery and he worked in IT, but they had no problem filling the air.

Things went better after that.

"Let's not see them again," Miles said later at the hotel. We were staying at a crappy Hilton in Midtown because it was what we could afford. "He's fucking dull. Does he just Charlie Brown his way through life?"

"They're working on his meds," I said. "Give the guy a break. He's brilliant."

"Didn't seem brilliant to me." Miles stuck his hand in my pants and I squirmed. "Seemed slow." He considered. "I liked his wife, though."

Of course Miles liked Lisa. I liked her too. I'd walked in that restaurant prepared to hate her, but she wasn't the monster I expected.

Now, the R train pulled up and we climbed on board. We had to take the local because it was the only one that stopped at Green-Wood. The R trains were the older cars, with orange and gold seats and sticky floors. "Don't touch that pole or you'll get a disease," Lisa said. She spread her feet wide like she was surfing. I grabbed the pole anyway. If there was a sudden stop, I didn't want to crush her. Standing next to her, I felt like the Jolly Green Giant.

I shouldn't have worn heels.

A pair of seats opened up and we made our move. Lisa sat gingerly on the seat next to me, staring curiously around the car. I put Paul on the seat between us so he'd be safe.

The train pulled away from the station, and the doors between cars burst open. It was the buskers. "Good afternoon ladies and gentlemen," he said. "We're students at LaGuardia majoring in music and dance, but in the summer we still got to eat. I hope I'm not disturbing you with my sounds." He launched into drumming for the next two minutes. Bicycle kid joined him and started to stunt, hopping on one wheel down the center aisle.

It was incredibly dangerous. I was grateful.

Just before we got to the next stop, the two boys walked up and down the aisle collecting money. I dropped in a dollar. "Thank you," he announced to the car before moving on. "Next time you see me, I'ma be more famous than you."

"That's not hard," I muttered.

Stand Clear of the Closing Doors, Please, the loudspeaker called, and the kids moved on to the next car.

Lisa watched them leave, then shook her head. "I'd forgotten what it's like, Brooklyn. I'm never here."

"Did you have to use your frequent flier miles?" I asked. That joke never got old as far as I was concerned.

She smiled vaguely. "Where do we get off again? I don't know any stops except Borough Hall. The only train I ever ride into Brooklyn is the IRT."

Figured. "Twenty-fifth Avenue," I answered. "Then we'll have to walk a couple of blocks." Through Sunset Park, but I didn't tell her that. Better to let her think we were still in the Slope.

"You know, we never came to Brooklyn," she said. "We had our own places."

"Prague?" I asked.

She nodded.

"And the flowers?"

"I thought he was still at home because it was just a business trip, but he popped out of nowhere when I returned to the hotel room full of flowers and asked me to marry him."

"That's ... romantic," I said. He'd told me this story too. His version was a lot less sweet.

She pulled out her phone and showed me some pictures. "We tried to go back once a year. He surprised me again last year, just when I thought we were done. Filled the room with flowers and asked to try again." She handed me the phone then, made me look at the flowers and the stupid happy grin on Paul's face.

He'd never said a word. Just told me one day that he was moving back in to give it one more chance and that he needed some space to make it work.

I sat with that a minute, but luckily I didn't have to say anything more because we were at our stop. We climbed the stairs and I was momentarily blinded. It was sunny, and the day was painfully beautiful. I figured out where we were and we directed her toward the gates.

She was quiet as we walked. "I wasn't sure about burying him in Brooklyn," she said finally. Her fingers fluttered over the braided handles. "But I know he wanted to be with his mother. That bitch."

Lisa wasn't wrong. He'd told me so, just before I left the country. He was feeling blue that day and I didn't know how to help him, so I took him to the cemetery because that always put me in a good mood. We walked for miles, all the way from Flatbush up to the Y to the Green-Wood Cemetery, the Gothic crown of King's County. He was proud of it, as only a native can be. "It's the second-biggest cemetery in the nation," he boasted. "The only one bigger is Arlington."

"Strange thing to be proud of."

"People used to come out here for picnics back in the day. They'd spend the whole day here and ride carriages up and down the paths."

I imagined it, carriage races through the crypts. "The Victorians really knew how to have a good time."

"Think about it," he said. "These flat ledgers make a nice spot for a picnic."

"How else are you going to see your relatives?" I asked.

We sat down on a nice flat one. The earliest date on the tombstone was 1887, a Clara Wainwright, aged 30. "Hiya, Clara," said Paul. "You lonely?"

"Not anymore," I said. "They're having a party up in there." There had to be fifteen names listed below Clara's. "What do you think they ate?"

"I know this one: fruits, sausages, cheese. You know we're not far from Coney Island."

"I'm not sure about the hot dogs, but I'm down with the cheese," I said.

He stood and leaped to the ground. "Oh," he said, and stopped dead in the middle of the path. "I forgot. I wrote you a poem on the train, as I flew to you like Woody Guthrie on the rails." He patted his pockets until he found his phone. "It's called 'Cheeses of Nazareth.'"

"Shut up," I said.

"It's the best thing I've ever written. I have high hopes for this piece."

He was never going to let me live down my midwestern roots. "I'm going to leave you right here," I said, but I would never.

"He walks on the waters of Lake ..." He stood on a bench, his hand over his heart.

"Michigan," I said. "Lake Michigan. You know, one of the Great Lakes?"

"Sure," Paul laughed. "Flyover country."

This time I did push him, and his phone went flying. I looked down. There was nothing on the screen. "Fool," I said.

He reached down and scooped it up. "Oh you tender ones, there are times when you should/ Enter into that breath which was not intended for you,/ Let Him part Himself on your cheese."

"No," I said. "That's disgusting."

"No? So dawn goes down today/Nothing gouda can stay."

"No gouda."

"Stop all the clocks/Turn off the provolone?"

I giggled as he leapt onto a bench. "Still no."

"Friends, Romans, Countrymen, lend me your cheddar," he shouted, the sun dappling across his face. He was joyful, unhinged.

He jumped down. "I think I've lost my always-tenuous grip on reality," he said.

"I'll say," I replied. He was impossible. Were his feet even on the ground? A cyclist rode up and set his bike against a tree, gathering dead flowers from a grave. It looked like serious stuff.

We calmed down and worked hard to do our best impression of responsible adults. He pretended to ignore us, but soon we grew tired of behaving.

"This way," said Paul. We turned the corner and found ourselves in a spot he recognized. "I think she's here." He chose Green-Wood as our next stop that day because he wanted to see his mother, and when we found her after thirty minutes of searching, in a wall on a half-remembered hill, he traced her name with his finger. Then he looked to his right. The adjacent spot was taken six months ago. "Damn," he said. "I should have bought it when I had the chance."

"Why's she here alone?" I asked. "Where's your father?"

He laughed. "Are you kidding? I wouldn't subject her to him for eternity." He looked at the wall. "Damn," he said again. He never cursed.

"Hey," I said. "You can get her moved. Buy a plot for yourself and Lisa, and move your mom."

"Yeah," he said, still fixated on the stone. "Although I'm only going to need two. Can you imagine Lisa allowing herself to be buried in Brooklyn?"

We walked around and picked a likely place where he could move her. You could see the gate from there, and he liked that.

"It's not all her fault," he said then. "I share the blame, too. That's what my therapist said. Two fundamentally nice people who don't know how to let each other down, so we keep on hurting each other."

"Don't look back," I said. "I'll help. I'll introduce you to people."

"I can't think of anything worse than meeting new people," he responded. Then, "Thank you for doing this with me," he said finally as we crossed into Prospect Park. We'd walked countless miles that perfect New York day. "This is one thing she'd never do."

He was always telling me about things she wouldn't do, and I drank that shit up.

"Thank you for coming with me," she said. "I didn't want to do this alone."

I nodded.

She'd made an appointment with the caretaker to get the lay of the land and make some decisions. "Is there someplace I can leave this?" She indicated the Barneys bag.

"This the ashes?" He peered inside and set it on his desk. "I like your bag. Old New York."

"You going to give us a discount?" I asked.

"Sure," he said. His name was Anthony, and he was the kind of rat-faced little man who wore nice suits and only treated women well when he was trying to sell them something. "I got deals." He had a minivan parked outside the office. We climbed in, with me in the backseat. He turned on the air conditioner, which I appreciated, but the air was a little musty.

"Not exactly a town car," Lisa observed.

"We only use the town car for services," he said. "Keeps it nice." She nodded. That was the kind of attention to detail she appreciated.

The caretaker drove us up to the same hill and I showed her the spot. It was exactly as I remembered. I backed off and let her have a moment with the monument. Oddly, the same cyclist as before rode up over the hill.

"That's not allowed," said Anthony. "Excuse me." He shouted and gestured at the cyclist, who stopped and started walking his bike. Anthony returned. "I catch him pulling that shit weekly," he muttered. "It's like the wild wild west out here."

I looked back at Lisa and realized that she was trying to get my attention. "I'd never have found this alone." She fingered the name carved into the marble and noticed the crowding problem immediately. "I'm going to need three spots together," she directed.

"We can do that," he said. "People resell real estate all the time here."

"Real estate?" I said, and he grinned. Obsequious little weasel. I wondered how much money he made selling graves. Was it a commission or salary thing? Commission probably.

Back at the office, Anthony solicitously showed Lisa to a chair. I trailed behind, but didn't sit down. Instead, I wandered over to the sales display against the wall. There was more variety than you'd think.

Anthony broke out his calculator. It had big buttons, and I was pretty sure it was just for show. "Let's see," he said, and started punching in numbers, then named a figure that would cover my rent for three months.

He glanced at our bag. "Do you want something nicer than that to fit inside the vault?"

"I don't know," she said. "It depends on how much." She turned to me. "Insurance isn't paying out."

"Why the hell not?" I said.

"They're calling it suspicious."

That was the first I'd heard of it. We all knew that it was accidental. He'd been having problems with his meds. They weren't working for the headaches; he'd told me so himself. "Do you want me to write a letter?"

"No," she said. "I've got his doctor doing that." She paused. "He'd sure as hell better, or I'll sue him for malpractice. He was the one who prescribed all that, after all."

"Like Michael Jackson," I said. "Or Prince."

Lisa grinned. "Can you imagine his face if he knew he'd been compared to Prince?"

But then Anthony was already pointing out the different urns and naming prices. "Do you take credit cards?" Lisa asked. She picked the one that could pay my rent for the rest of the year.

"You're okay getting to the airport?" Paul asked. We'd left the cemetery and were wending our way through Prospect Park.

I said he shouldn't worry; I always took care of myself.

He stopped in the middle of the path. "That's not fair," he said. "You know I'd do anything for you."

I laughed a little and pulled him along. "Of course you would." He'd moved back in with Lisa about a year before, and this was the first time I'd seen him in months. The last thing I wanted to do was argue.

"No," he said. "No. You don't understand. You're one of three people in the entire city who cares about me."

"Don't be ridiculous," I said. "People love you. You are loved."

He blew out a long breath. "I've been sleeping on the sofa. For a month, I've been sleeping on the sofa."

I wanted to remind him that he wouldn't be sleeping on my sofa, but we weren't in that place anymore and instead I said that if he wanted, he could stay at my apartment while I was gone. "Just don't kill my plants," I added.

To his credit, he did think about it for a minute.

"So?" I asked, holding my breath.

"No," he said finally. "I'm going to keep trying. She's trying, so I should, too."

I didn't have cell service when I was in Dublin. It was all I could do to pay for the trip, so I figured I'd just get by, and it mostly worked out. I just connected to WiFi when I could and went incognito the rest of the time.

I rented a little motorbike and scootered my way around the country, paying cash and connecting to the land as much as possible and depending on library computer labs and the occasional hotel. We emailed often as I moved about the country rooting through libraries and I didn't miss him because he was always there.

So I wrote him long emails describing my experience and my research and he asked me questions that nudged me along when I was stuck and anytime I asked him how he was, he demurred, "The Earth gives forth." I was pretty sure he was quoting something.

The day I found out, there was a message from him at the top of my Inbox. There was another message from Lisa at the bottom. I knew immediately that something was wrong.

I read his message first. He was fine, he said, and he gave me a list of questions about my travels. Nothing about his message said he wouldn't be there to get my reply. So I replied. I replied, and I answered every one of his questions. It probably took me two hours to write him everything, and at the end I told him I was coming home in two weeks and he didn't need to start over because he could start with me. I pressed Send.

Then I skipped Lisa's message so I could pretend for a little longer that everything was fine.

Anthony discreetly ran her credit card, then went into the back to formalize the paperwork. Lisa turned to me. "I found him, you know."

I did know. I'd heard it from a mutual friend in the days immediately following. I couldn't come back early because I didn't qualify for a bereavement fare.

"He was face down at his desk. There was vomit all over his laptop. Pills."

I pictured their apartment, the whole scene. I didn't want to know this.

"I was sleeping," she said. "Sleeping, while he was dying."

"It was an accident," I said.

"I didn't even notice that he hadn't come to bed. Why didn't I hear?"

I almost told her that I knew why, but we'd gotten so good at pretending, why ruin it now? "How could you know?" I said instead.

I'd have known.

Anthony returned with the paperwork, she signed the receipt, and I handed over the bag. Lisa paused at the door. "I'd like to take a little bit of him home," she said, and Anthony obliged, cracking open the box and scooping some ashes into a paper bag. She stuck it in her pocket and waved goodbye.

"Perhaps I'll spread it somewhere," she said. "Prague, maybe."

"Sure," I said.

Lisa stuck the receipt in her purse and turned to look back at the gates. "That man never shopped at Barney's a day in his life."

We made our way to the subway. "I hope you understand," she said. "When we do the graveside, it'll be family only."

I'd call his sister for details. I had no intention of being kept away.

The train stopped at Borough Hall. "Do you want to get brunch?" she asked next.

"Sure," I said. "You buying?"

❧❦❧

ADVICE TO A YOUNG WOMAN
by Mary Christine Kane

No one is watching you. No one *knows*.

It's true what they say about happiness being about the glasses. Although I don't much like the H word because of its corollary. Happiness can be trying a new hairstyle, getting the splinter out. Sadness can salt your days for a lifetime.

It's easy to name villains, a word I don't like much because of its corollary. People who make good news are heroes. Villain comes from the benign "farmhand." It wasn't necessary to create a whole new word for women who are heroes and then later name a drug after it. Hero also means very long sandwich.

You were waiting for me to grip you with some surprising happiness. You, who resist gripping, I'm sorry. The secret is: nobody *knows*.

Do not lend out your favorite books. Check if there's toilet paper before you unzip.

When your heart is burning, burning, put on some red lipstick and be a dragon. Wait until the conflagration makes your landscape glow again.

❧◉◞

MEN O PAUSE
by Lori Levy

Men, oh please, would you pause for a minute
while we women catch our breath?
We have entered a fun-house of stretch and distortion
where glass cracks our skin and loosens our muscles
till we sag and bulge, spilling out of ourselves.
We would run to escape, but there's no way out.

Pause oh men while we slip back in
to our faces and figures, softened, ripened.
We need time to adjust; to learn how to wear
these new women in our mirrors.
Let us zigzag for a while,
    hot cold, out of whack,
till we find our way back to
beautiful, sexual.
Or not.

Oh, women, pause.
Perhaps we've got it all wrong: this isn't a fun-house,
just a room we have entered, empty at the moment.
Should we leave it as it is? Open, undefined.
Put pillows on the floor? Chocolate in bowls?
We could fill the space with jasmine, if we want.
Or just invite someone in—like the man
we left stranded in the fun-house.
The one we menopaused.

༄☯☯༄

LATCH LATCH LATCH
by Susan Calvillo

my friends, other mothers, & experts say: latch, latch, latch, just keep latching. it'll happen eventually. it'll happen naturally. it doesn't. & it doesn't. & it's easy to think: I must be unnatural. I'm missing something. something must be wrong with me. none of my self-help books explain: how to prepare for failure. why would they? *can't*-help books don't sell. I search for other real-life survival guides. they're hard to find. on breastfeeding forums, mamas only post success stories: photos of their babies swinging by their lips from their glorious tits. like me, other failures are too shy to post their situation. the few that do, don't get likes or comments. their posts get buried. the breastfeeding community refuses to acknowledge failure. refuses to accept this could happen.

you must not be doing it right.   *you don't want it enough.* the
feedings blur. the days   blur. I lose the ability to
think straight. to   make informed
decisions. I am   aware, but I
cannot correct   course. I know I
should find a   lactation
consultant,   but the free
services at   my hospital
are closed   due to covid,
my eyes are   too blurry to
read new   names off
the screen,   the
voicemails are   full for the
few that offer   virtual
sessions. I know   I should stop
offering the bottle. I   hear what they say:
starve them a little,   *they'll get the idea.* but
our babies are already too   small, & if they get smaller,

we'll have to go back to the hospital. even in normal times no one wants a trip to the hospital. I hear about using preemie nipples on bottles to slow the flow, *place the interest back on the breast.* my sister offers to pick them up for me, but between the hoarding & looting, the pharmacy & target shelves are all empty. so she picks up a variety pack from the pet store: for puppies, kitties, bunnies, & ferrets. she has braved 5+ stores to give me this option. I don't want to let her down by saying *thanks*, but *no thanks*. I stare through the plastic & think these nipples look nothing like my nipples. if for some reason the babies like the shape of a ferret's nipples more than mine then I'll never convince them to switch to the breast. I wait a torturous 24 hours (a combined 22 feedings) for nipples shaped like mine to arrive in the mail. the new nipples work okay for one baby, but the other grows lethargic, detached, & confused. I realize fulfilling the dream of breastfeeding isn't worth this misery. *yes, it is*, my friends, other mothers, the experts, the self-help books, the survival guides, the success stories, the photos of glorious tits say. think about the *health benefits*. think about the *bond* with your baby. not *baby*, I say, *babies*. & I give up. & it's the best thing I've ever done for them. it's the decision that kept them alive.   *- confession*

"Walk with Me" by Karen Boissonneault-Gauthier

THE HOPE TREE
by Shaindel Beers

The man always leaves an apple on the nightstand. Mirah knows this is his idea of kindness. Something in addition to the stack of bills he pins under the bedside lamp. Today, she devours the apple, core and all—save for the one seed she pushes into the earth. She wants the pain of the stem stuck in her throat but also the hope of a tree outside her window.

The next day, a miracle. A pink-blossomed tree reaches into the clouds. My escape, she thinks. She climbs, slick sandal soles sliding over bark. She lets her sandals fall and hears the satisfying thump-thump of them hitting the ground below her. The rough bark of the tree reminds her of her barefoot life as a girl. She wonders if the man always knew that his apples were magical. If he was a genie of some sort. She thinks of all the apples she has wasted since he has been coming to her, like clockwork once a week since his wife died. At least, this is the story he has always told her. He is so lonely. So lonely since the death of his wife. And she has had no reason to doubt him.

She thinks of his acrid sweat. His hairy belly above her. The way she always turns her face so he can't kiss her mouth. Sometimes she would give one of his apples to an orphan sweeping the street for change and wickedly think, "Ah, someone who is less fortunate than I am." Another time, she saved the apples in her cupboard until she had enough to make a cake for a man she hoped might marry her. Instead, she will always remember how mournful he looked when she set the cake on the table.

"Mirah, I cannot accept this present from you. You are a prostitute and can be nothing more to me." After that night, she never saw him again.

But now a city in the clouds—all in this mysterious apple tree. A small house sits at the top of each branch. Wondrous little cottages in bright pinks, yellows, blues, greens. All of the women wave at her. They sweep their doorsteps as she walks by. Come out to cool pies on their porch railings. *What is this place?* she finally asks. *Whore Heaven? Prostitute paradise?* Some women smile and nod. She wants to deny them, to say she doesn't belong here, but it is true. Ever since her father died, since her brother ran away with the inheritance, she has been a *whore*. She whispers the word to herself now, a spell, a charm, an enchantment. It seemed the only choice to make, and then—no going back.

You can come and go as you please, a young girl says. She is so young, Mirah wants to fall to her knees and hug the girl, but she doesn't want to shame her. How old is she? Ten? Eleven? *But tell no one, or the spell will be broken for you,* the girl continues.

She finds her little house already set up for her. Daisies in the front yard. White summer curtains with a small strawberry print billow out the window. Why would anyone leave?

Some miss their families, a woman in purple says. *Others miss men.* Mirah ponders this. Gruff barking voices, the smell of their skin. Will she miss them? She explores her quaint kitchen. She can't imagine needing anything else. There is a small, clean oven, a set of white ceramic mixing bowls, cast iron pots and pans. She sits on the edge of her bed next to a cozy fireplace. Next to it, a small table. On the table, an apple, shiny and red.

෧෨

AUTHOR BIOS

Rahne Alexander is an intermedia artist and writer. Her essay collection, *Heretic to Housewife*, won the 2019 OutWrite Nonfiction Chapbook Prize. She lives in Baltimore, Maryland with her spouse and their cats, Laverne and Shirley. More: www.rahne.com

Joel Allegretti is the author of, most recently, *Platypus* (NYQ Books, 2017), a collection of poems, prose, and performance texts, and *Our Dolphin* (Thrice Publishing, 2016), a novella. His second book of poems, *Father Silicon* (The Poet's Press, 2006), was selected by *The Kansas City Star* as one of 100 Noteworthy Books of 2006. He is the editor of *Rabbit Ears: TV Poems* (NYQ Books, 2015). *The Boston Globe* called *Rabbit Ears* "cleverly edited" and "a smart exploration of the many, many meanings of TV." *Rain Taxi* said, "With its diversity of content and poetic form, *Rabbit Ears* feels more rich and eclectic than any other poetry anthology on the market."

Cecilia Baader is a reader, writer, and a teacher, not necessarily in that order. She's as Chicago as they come, and her words appear in Ink Pot and Outlook India. She is currently working on a novel.

Shaindel Beers is the author of three full-length poetry collections, *A Brief History of Time* (2009) and *The Children's War and Other Poems* (2013), both from Salt Publishing, and most recently *Secure Your Own Mask* (2018), which was the winner of the White Pine Press Poetry Prize and a finalist for the Oregon Book Award. She teaches at Blue Mountain Community College in Pendleton, Oregon. Learn more at http://shaindelbeers.com.

Wendy Besel Hahn earned her MFA from George Mason University. She attended Bread Loaf Writers' Conference as a nonfiction contributor in 2016. Her work appears in *The Washington Post, Scary Mommy, Redivider, Sojourners*, and elsewhere. She is the nonfiction editor for *Furious Gravity: Vol. IX* in Grace and Gravity Series (May 2020), founded by Richard Peabody and edited by Melissa Scholes Young. She recently relocated from the Metro Washington D.C. area to Denver, Colorado, closer to her roots.

Susan Calvillo is a Chinese/Mexican-American and the author of *Excerpts from My Grocery List* (Beard of Bees). Her writing appears in *Zyzzyva, New American Writing, Nightmare Magazine, Parenting Stories Gone Speculative*, and other charming magazines. By day, she's a production editor, publishing non-fiction texts in the medical, education, and tech industries. She copy edits for *Foglifter*, a journal created by and for LGBTQ+ writers and readers, with an emphasis on publishing those multi-marginalized (BIPOC, youth, elders, and people with disabilities). And she's a Chapter 510 mentor for BIPOC LGBTQ+ Oakland youth writing Sci-Fi/Fantasy.

Kathryn de Lancellotti's chapbook *Impossible Thirst* was published June 2020, Moon Tide Press. She is a Pushcart Prize nominee and a former recipient of the George Hitchcock Memorial Poetry Prize. Her poems and other works have appeared in *Thrush, Rust + Moth, The Night Heron Barks, The American Journal of Poetry, Quarterly West*, and others. She received her MFA in Creative Writing from Sierra Nevada University and resides on the Central Coast, California, with her family.

Heather Fowler is a magical realist, poet, screenwriter, and novelist, whose brand is Sexy Monsters, Killer Women. Of her work, the *New York Times* says she offers a "bright and affectionate vision of mystical worlds" and "great ideas and characters." Fowler's *People with Holes* was a finalist for the Foreword Reviews Book of the Year Award in Short Fiction. Her stories and poems have been published online and in print in the U.S., England, Australia, and India. She is an avid podcaster on the craft of writing and recently completed a TFT Professional Program in Screenwriting at UC Los Angeles. She is co-CEO of Hot Redhead Media, a company that champions women and diverse authors, and lives in San Diego with her kids and two ornery cats Poem Charlie and Rorschach. Lately, she's working on screenplays and novels. Drop her a line.

Allison Fradkin delights in applying her Women's & Gender Studies education to the creation of satirically scintillating stories for the stage. Scriptly speaking, her plays (sur)pass the Bechdel Test and enlist their characters in a caricature of the idiocies and intricacies of insidious isms. Allison's short plays have been presented by Accidental Shakespeare Company, Almost Adults Productions, American Blues Theater, Broken Nose Theatre, Clutch Productions, Dragon Productions, Experimental Theatre Cooperative, Kansas City Public Theatre, The Kennedy Center, The Majestic Theatre, Muhlenberg College, Ophelia's Jump Productions, Play Club West, StageQ, The Tank, UNO Theatre, and the Women's Theatre Festival. She has also written a full-length feminist musical tribute to The Golden Girls, which will make its debut with Queer Theatre Kalamazoo later this year. An enthusiast of inclusivity and accessibility, Fradkin freelances for her hometown of Chicago as Literary Manager of Violet Surprise Theatre, curating new works by queer women; and as Dramatist for Special Gifts Theatre, adapting scripts for actors of all abilities.

Avital Gad-Cykman is the author of *Light Reflection Over Blues* (Ravenna Press) and *Life In, Life Out* (Matter Press). She is the winner of Margaret Atwood Studies Magazine Prize and The Hawthorne Citation Short Story Contest, twice a finalist for the Iowa Fiction Award and a six-time nominee for the Pushcart. Her stories appear in *Spectrum, The Dr. Eckleburg Review, Iron Horse, Prairie Schooner, Ambit, McSweeney's Quarterly* and *Michigan Quarterly,* twice in *Best Short Fictions, W.W. Norton's Flash Fiction International* anthology and elsewhere. She holds a Ph.D. in English Literature, focused on minorities, gender and trauma, and lives in Brazil.

Cynthia Gallaher, a Chicago-based poet and visual artist, is author of four poetry collections, many with themes, including *Epicurean Ecstasy:*

More Poems About Food, Drink, Herbs and Spices, and three chapbooks, including Drenched. Her nonfiction/memoir/creativity guide *Frugal Poets' Guide to Life: How to Live a Poetic Life, Even If You Aren't a Poet* won a National Indie Excellence Award. Follow her on Twitter at @ swimmerpoet, Instagram at @frugalpoet and her Facebook page at @ frugalpoets. Amazon Author Page: http://bit.ly/gallaherc Website: http://bit.ly/cynthiagallaher.

Samm Genesee is pursuing an MFT at Antioch, and has an MFA in poetry from SF State. She runs an experiential arts retreat called, Dream Factory Workshops, and has previously worked facilitating films and poetry workshops at, Turning Point Shelter, in collaboration with the nonprofit, Women's Voices Now. She makes (audio) poetry and comics that can be found published in various places such as, *Nokturno, Huffington Post,* and *Everyday Genius.* For fun, she likes to do sand play therapy in cafes or in her living room with friends. "Not knowing is most intimate" —Dizang, from a Zen Koan

Tanya (Hyonhye) Ko Hong (고현혜) is a bilingual Korean American poet, translator, playwright, and cultural curator. She has an MFA in Creative Writing from Antioch University, Los Angeles. Tanya was the first Korean American recipient of the Yun Doon-ju Korean American Literature Award, the 10th Ko Won Memorial Foundation Literature Award, the Dritëro Agolli award at the International Korçare Poetry Festival, and has been nominated for a Pushcart Prize.Her most recent collection, *The War Still Within* (2019, KYSO Flash) includes a well-researched and vividly imagined sequence of poems based on the experiences of the Korean "Comfort Woman," and received an honorable mention from the Women's National Book Association. She expanded it into a play which was previewed by Tabula RaSa at the NYC Theater and Performance Lab.

Babo Kamel's work appears in publications such as the *Lily Poetry Review, Greensboro Review, Painted Bride Quarterly, CV2, Poet Lore,* and *Best Canadian Poetry 2020.* She holds an MFA from Warren Wilson's Program for

Writers. She is a Best of Net nominee, and a six-time Pushcart nominee, Her chapbook, *After*, is published with Finishing Line Press Find her at: www.babokamel.com.

Mary Christine Kane grew up in Buffalo, New York and has spent her adult life in the Twin Cities of Minnesota. She works in marketing and is a volunteer for the arts, parks, and animal rescue. Her poetry has appeared in numerous journals and anthologies including *Bluestem; The Buffalo Anthology, Right Here, Right Now; Ponder Review* and others. Her poetry chapbook, *Between the stars where you are lost*, was published in 2019 by Finishing Line Press. Mary can be found online at marychristinekane.com.

Jen Knox teaches at Ohio State University and is the founder of Unleash Creatives. Jen has taught creative writing for over a decade and combines her love of creativity with personal development and leadership in work-shops she hosts around the world. Her debut novel, *We Arrive Uninvited*, is the Prose Award winner from Steel Toe Books, and her collection of climate fiction, *The Glass City*, won the Press Americana Prize for Prose. Jen's shorter work appears in over a hundred journals and magazines, including *McSweeney's Internet Quarterly, The Saturday Evening Post, Chicago Review, and Chicago Tribune*, among others. She recently won the 2023 CutBank Montana Prize in Nonfiction and is finalizing a collection of essays about work. jenknox.com

Lori Levy's poems have appeared in *Rattle, Nimrod International Journal, Poet Lore, Mom Egg Review, Paterson Literary Review*, and numerous other literary journals and anthologies in the U.S., the U.K., and Israel. Her work has also been published in medical humanities journals. Her chapbook, "What Do You Mean When You Say Green? and Other Poems of Color," has just been published by Kelsay Books, and she has another chapbook forthcoming from Ben Yehuda Press. Lori lives with her extended family in Los Angeles, but "home" has also been Vermont and Israel and, for several months, Panama while visiting her son and granddaughters.

Traci McMickle (she/her/hers) is a bi/pan/queer poet from Montana, where she lives with a spouse and an incorrigible Rottweiler. Traci has an MFA from the University of New Orleans. Her work is published in *Rattle, Chaotic Merge Magazine, Eternal Haunted Summer, Plainsongs, Typehouse Literary Magazine,* and *Panoply.*

Galel A. Medina is a Central American queer folk horror author who finds inspiration in the myths and legends that have been passed down through generations. Her work is influenced by the Latin American tradition of Magical Realism and uses fantastical elements to highlight the complexities of queerness and gender in this cultural area. She is currently writing a novel with the aid of copious amounts of matcha and too many playlists. Based some twenty miles from the Caribbean, Galel lives on a busy street surrounded by fruit trees, cheese vendors, and her many pets.

Marisca Pichette is a queer author based in Massachusetts, on Pocumtuck and Abenaki land. Her work has appeared in *Room Magazine, Flash Fiction Online, Necessary Fiction,* and *Plenitude Magazine,* among others. She is the winner of the 2022 F(r)iction Spring Literary Contest and has been nominated for the Best of the Net, Pushcart, Utopia, and Dwarf Stars awards. Their debut poetry collection, *Rivers in Your Skin, Sirens in Your Hair,* is out now from Android Press. Find them on Twitter as @MariscaPichette, Instagram as @marisca_write, and BlueSky as @marisca.bsky.social.

Leslie Pietrzyk's collection of linked stories set in DC, *Admit This to No One,* was published in 2021 by Unnamed Press. Her first collection of stories, *This Angel on My Chest,* won the 2015 Drue Heinz Literature Prize. Short fiction and essays have appeared in, among others, *Ploughshares, Story Magazine, Hudson Review, Southern Review, Gettysburg Review, Iowa Review, The Sun, Cincinnati Review,* and *The Washington Post Magazine.* Awards include a Pushcart Prize in 2020.

Leigh Camacho Rourks is a Cuban-American author living and working in Central Florida, where she is an Assistant Professor at Beacon College. She won the St. Lawrence Book Award for her debut story collection, *Moon Trees and Other Orphans*, which, among other accolades, received a starred review from *Kirkus Reviews*. She is also the recipient of the Glenna Luschei Prairie Schooner Award and the Robert Watson Literary Review Prize, and her work has been shortlisted for several other awards. *Digital Voices*, her new book on Creative Writing Pedagogy is now available from Bloomsbury Publishing.

Marivi Soliven has authored 17 books and taught creative writing at the University of the Philippines, Diliman and at UC San Diego. She was awarded a Hedgebrook writing residency in 2018. Her debut novel *The Mango Bride* won the Grand Prize at the 2011 Carlos Palanca Memorial Awards for Literature, the Philippine counterpart of the Pulitzer Prize and the San Diego Book Awards. A film adaptation is in process. The film version of her story "Pandemic Bread," published in the San Diego Decameron Project, has screened at festivals in LA, Philadelphia and San Diego.

ARTIST BIOS

Cynthia Yatchman is a Seattle based artist and art instructor. A former ceramicist, she received her B.F.A. in painting (UW). She switched from 3D to 2D and has remained there ever since. She works primarily on paintings, prints, and collages. Her art is housed in numerous public and private collections. She has exhibited on both coasts, extensively in the Northwest, including shows at Seattle University, SPU, Shoreline Community College, the Tacoma and Seattle Convention Centers and the PaciNic Science Center. She is a member of the Seattle Print Art Association, Puget Sound Painters of the Northwest, and Center of Contemporary Art.

David Sheskin is an artist and writer whose work has appeared in numerous magazines over the years. Most recently he has appeared in *Cleaver Magazine, Quarterly West, Shenandoah* and *Chicago Quarterly Review.* His most recent books are *Art That Speaks, David Sheskin's Cabinet of Curiosities* and *Outrageous Wedding Announcements.*

Karen Boissonneault-Gauthier is a Stittsville, Ontario Indigenous writer and photographer. Her images are produced intuitively using digital photography. As an internationally published person, she cuts her teeth creating written and visual works for the best companies, corporate magazines and literary publications. Karen has been nominated "Best of the Net" artist for 2022.

Kelsey Bryan-Zwick (she/they) is a queer, disabled, bilingual immigrant, author and artist based in Los Angeles, California. Their debut poetry collection, *Here Go the Knives* (Moon Tide Press 2022)—part memoir, part magical realism, part illustration—focuses on their decades surviving with debilitating scoliosis. In 2021, Kelsey's fourth chapbook, *Bone Water*, which also centers on disability, was published by Blanket Sea Press as their Advocacy and Awareness project. Kelsey is The Poetry Lab's Lead Collaborating Fellow and a Los Angeles Poet Society organizing. Kelsey is a UC Santa Cruz alum (go banana slugs!) and their poetry has twice been nominated for the Pushcart Prize, as well for the Best of the Net. On the gram @theexquisitepoet and on the web www.kelseybryanzwick. wixsite.com/poetry.

OTHER TITLES FROM HOT REDHEAD MEDIA:

ELEGANTLY NAKED
IN MY SEXY
MENTAL ILLNESS

HEATHER FOWLER
STORIES

Heather Fowler's fourth collection of short fiction speaks to the language of need. Desperate, obsessive, and even demented need is voiced by characters ill or ill-advised. From modern to historical, cyber to stalker, explicit to tender, the relationships in Elegantly Naked in My Sexy Mental Illness translate love and lust into intimate disorder. How we hear our own need and the way it sounds to others proves, in this addictive collection, an imperfect but utterly captivating conversation.

a novel

"A DAGGER-SHARP STUDY OF ADDICTION, OBSESSION, AND SELF-DESTRUCTION,
WRAPPED IN A MYSTERIOUS GLOAM OF THE SUPERNATURAL." -JEFFREY THOMAS

MICHAEL TAKEDA

A group of personable, young, gay heroin addicts in Urbino, Italy have enough problems, but when their American guest, resident poet Moth connects with a golden stranger and his shared affliction, a narrative about everyday lives riddled with addictions turns into one exploring a brutally destructive pursuit of sex as a compulsion, coupled with sociopathological transformation. A novel both literary and evocative of the traditional horror or vampire genres, Takeda's Moth straddles the real and the surreal brilliantly, making its own dark magic for readers on the page.